Fastlander Fury

(Fastlanders, Book 1)

T. S. JOYCE

Fastlander Fury

ISBN: 9798322774587
Copyright © 2024, T. S. Joyce
First electronic publication: April 2024

T. S. Joyce
www. tsjoyce.com

All Rights Are Reserved. No part of this book may be used or reproduced in any manner whatsoever without written permission, except in the case of brief quotations embodied in critical articles and reviews. The unauthorized reproduction or distribution of this copyrighted work is illegal. No part of this book may be scanned, uploaded or distributed via the Internet or any other means, electronic or print, without the author's permission.

NOTE FROM THE AUTHOR:

This book is a work of fiction. The names, characters, places, and incidents are products of the writer's imagination or have been used fictitiously and are not to be construed as real. Any resemblance to persons, living or dead, actual events, locale or organizations is entirely coincidental. The author does not have any control over and does not assume any responsibility for third-party websites or their content.

Published in the United States of America

First digital publication: April 2024
First print publication: April 2024

DEDICATION

For those butter cookies in the tins our parents used to store sewing kits in. How did I not know these cookies were so delicious until my 41st year of life?
I've had them for breakfast six days in a row.

This book is dedicated to you, Butter Cookies.

ACKNOWLEDGMENTS

A special thank you to my husband, who runs this house like a well-oiled machine on the weeks that the books consume me. And to my kiddos and step-kiddos, who cheer on a mother/step-mother who lives half her life in the real world, and half lost in her imagination. This is the team that motivates me to work to be the best version of myself. The books are possible because of the quiet work they do behind the scenes to keep myself, my work, and our family headed in the right direction.

Total MVPs.

ONE

Gunner would've ridden his motorcycle all night if he hadn't been running on fumes.

No help for it, he had to stop for gas.

He eased into a gas station on the outskirts of Laramie, Wyoming. He'd been trying to escape Damon's Mountains for weeks, but he just kept circling Saratoga. His damn inner grizzly had issues and wouldn't leave territory he'd claimed as his.

Gunner pulled his wallet out of his back pocket and did a quick scan of the station. There were two cars parked up by the door. One silver Civic that still looked wet from a car wash, which made sense because there was a wash-by-hand joint next door. The other car was a beat-up old truck that would've drawn a smile to his face if he had a heart. It was the same model his dad drove.

At one of the pumps, there was a black truck with dark-tinted windows. A man was talking on the phone inside. His sensitive shifter hearing picked up bits and pieces of the conversation.

"...how should I know?..."

"...what do you want me to do about it..."

"...I don't know, you're the one tracking her..."

"...she's talking to the guy behind the counter..."

It was that last part that dragged his attention back to the black truck. He could barely make out the outline of the man from here. He had a visor over his helmet to shield his face from the world, and the dark tint on the man's front windshield was not legal at all.

The man was quiet, head turned toward the gas station—that much Gunner could see.

He put his credit card in the slot and settled the gas nozzle into his tank. God, it was a good thing he had stopped. He was nearly dry.

Inside the gas station, a woman was paying for some snacks. Skittles, a bag of potato chips, a Sprite...nice.

All he could see was her back, but she had long

brunette hair that had been curled into soft waves. She wore a baggy neon-pink hoodie that hung down to her hips and cutoff jean shorts—the kind with the white strings hanging down the curves of her thighs. Nice ass. Pretty figure. She had a tattoo of some kind of bird with outstretched wings on the back of her thigh, partially hidden by her shorts. She wore a backwards hat on her head. Looked comfy.

"...yeah, she's wearing those shorts you hate again..."

Gunner's snarl kicked up, and he was glad for the helmet. It hid most of the sound. What was this dude's problem?

"...want me to follow her?..."

He was so distracted, Gunner nearly flooded gasoline over the lip of his tank. He clicked it off and cursed when the nozzle dripped a few drops onto the black paint of his Ducati. He quickly wiped it off with the hem of his black T-shirt.

"...she won't notice me..."

Another snarl ripped out of Gunner. He needed to get out of here before he throttled this guy and flipped his truck.

He slid his leg over the seat and started the bike,

but he couldn't make himself leave.

Fuck.

The roaring in his ears was so loud, and he was going to explode. Everything was a trigger now. He hated…hated…*hated* being himself.

He squeezed the grips of his motorcycle, but the tension was only building. The damn bear was doing something strange.

Gunner angled his head toward the gas station again. That woman was being watched, and from her easygoing nature as she laughed with the gas station attendant, she didn't have any idea.

"This isn't my problem," he snarled out softly, but the responding growl said his animal disagreed. "Well, what are you gonna fuckin' do?" Gunner blurted, sitting up straight. "You gonna save her? You're worse than that guy could be." Another growled response, and he wanted to scream at the dark sky and curse the stars.

Fine. Gunner slid off the motorcycle. "Kill him then. See if I care. Maybe Damon will finally be pushed into putting me down."

But when he tried to make his way to the truck, his legs went a different direction. Now he was walking toward the damn gas station.

No, no, no, no.

Gunner tried to stop, but as always, it was no use. He wasn't in control on a good day, and as usual, this wasn't a good day.

Resigned to his fate, or perhaps defeated, he hoped she would make it to her car before he could reach her. She was at the door already, her back to the glass there, head turned as she said something to the cashier. No luck on her getting out of his way, she turned just as he reached for the handle.

Gunner startled to a stop and froze.

The woman was in her early thirties, perhaps. Her eyebrows were dark like her hair, and delicately arched in surprise as she laid those pretty hazel eyes on him. She had full lips and a nose that was cute enough, but looked as if it had been broken and healed rough. It did nothing to take away from her pretty eyes or her striking bone structure.

"Let me," she said, pushing the door open for him. She held it and waited for him to pass.

Slowly, he walked through the open doorway and looked down at her. She was perhaps five-foot-five—a full foot shorter than him.

She glanced out at the gas pumps, then back to him. He'd just frozen inside the gas station like a dumbass.

"I like your bike," she said softly.

"You shouldn't talk to strangers," he growled.

Her eyes went wide at the sound of his voice. She shrank back and dropped her gaze. Mmm. Submissive.

"H-have a good night," she uttered.

"See you later, Hallie," the cashier called.

Hallie lifted her hand in a two-fingered wave.

This was the part where Gunner should let her go, let her live her life and figure her shit out.

But the black truck caught his attention. It pulled forward and parked next to the silver Civic, and if Gunner had to guess, he would say that was her car.

"Do you know that truck?" he asked just before the door swung closed.

She lurched for the handle, missed, and apologized. To the door? He didn't understand submissives. Their personalities were pitiful to him.

She opened the door again, and asked, "Did you say something?"

Gunner placed his hands in front of himself and

lifted his chin higher into the air. "Do you know that truck?" he repeated.

She looked out the window at the black pickup. "I don't think so. Why?"

Gunner angled his head and cracked his neck. What was he doing here? He should be on the open road trying to figure out what he would do next. "You should wait for him to leave before you get into your car."

"Okay. Okay, you're scaring me," she admitted softly, and he could tell from the tone of her voice she was telling the truth.

He stifled an eye roll. "Where are you going after this?"

"Why do you care?"

"I don't. I literally don't care about anything. I don't even know why I'm standing here having this conversation right now."

She frowned and glanced back at the black truck. "Did he get gas?" she asked the cashier.

"Nope. He's just been sitting there," the cashier said. "I'm watching him on the video monitor. He has his window open, but all I can see is his elbow. He looks like he has a phone up to his ear."

"Can you turn the video off for a few minutes?" Gunner asked.

The cashier just stared at him for a few seconds. "Why?"

Gunner checked the cameras inside. "So I can clear the lot so the lady can leave."

The dark-haired cashier's eyebrows shot upward. The corners of his mouth turned down as if he was considering it. A few seconds later, he shook his head. "My boss will know."

Gunner nodded once. "Fuck it. If a guy named Damon calls here asking about this, just tell him it's exactly who he thinks it is."

Gunner yanked the door open and told Hallie to, "Stay put."

She did not stay put. She followed him right out toward the truck. Humans had terrible survival instincts sometimes.

Well, whatever.

"What are you doing?" the man in the truck asked as Gunner rounded the front end. He was still holding the phone, and it was the first good look Gunner got of his face. The man had brown hair that hung down to his clean-shaven jawline, dark eyes, and a scar from his lip to his jaw. He was wearing a flannel. He wasn't wearing a seatbelt, so Gunner didn't bother with opening the door. He reached in, grabbed him by the front of his shirt, and yanked that man out through the open window.

Fuckface screamed loud enough to make Gunner's sensitive ears ring, and once again he was glad for the helmet. That could've been way worse.

"You know him?" Gunner asked Hallie, who was standing up on the sidewalk, hunched in on herself like she was trying to make herself small. "Stand up straight," he barked, and with a whimper, she did. "Who is he?"

"I...I don't know."

"Okay, he was talking to someone on the phone about your clothes. Who would hate those shorts you're wearin'?"

Her eyes went wide and her face went blank, and that right there said she knew who he was talking about.

"Why is this man tracking you?"

The man struggled in his arms, so Gunner threw him on the ground, balled his fist, and cracked him twice against the jaw. He went limp, and groaned.

"Another one will kill you, asshole. I'll put my fist right through your skull. Don't tempt me."

Gunner stood back up. "Who's tracking you?"

"My ex," Hallie whispered. "He hated if I wore my shorts in public."

The booming of a gun deafened Gunner, and a high-pitched whining sounded in his ears as pain shredded through his arm.

That dumb-fuck had a handgun.

Gunner huffed a laugh and ducked the next discharged bullet. There was a screeching sound in the background, but all he could see was red. Gunner grabbed the man's wrist and snapped it. The gun clattered to the ground as the man yelled in pain, but Gunner wasn't done. He picked up the weapon, took it apart completely, and let the pieces clatter to the ground. He picked the man up and held him in the air, then flipped his helmet visor open so this asshole could see his glowing eyes before he died. The man was babbling in fear. Gunner bunched his muscles to throw him into the brick wall hard enough to take his life.

Just as he moved to throw him, Gunner's body froze as electricity zinged through him, and he staggered backward stiffly. His hand wouldn't hold the man anymore.

Hallie was tasing him. She was tasing him and yelling something he couldn't understand.

"Stop," he gritted out.

The man dropped to the ground, stunned as well, and Gunner tried to break away from the electric charge.

She yanked the Taser back, and Gunner stumbled back a few steps.

He felt betrayed.

"You have to go," she murmured, panic infusing her words.

"Why?" he gritted out. "Why did you do that?"

"Because I heard what you said in there! You said Damon's name, and your eyes say you aren't human. Robby!" she yelled.

"Yeah?" the cashier asked from the open doorway.

"Delete that footage."

"But my boss—"

"I'm begging you. I'll owe you a favor. Just delete it. Please."

Robby blinked twice, and then nodded. "Okay."

He disappeared inside, and Hallie stooped and picked up the man's cracked phone from the pavement. She lifted it to her ear. "Are you still there?"

With his visor lifted, Gunner could hear the other end of the conversation plain as day. "I haven't heard your voice in awhile. I—"

"Shut the fuck up, Derek. I'm calling the police."

"Hallie, wait!"

She hung up. Eyes full of angry tears, she looked up at Gunner. "You have to go."

"You tased me," he growled, still pissed.

"I know who Damon is."

"How do you know him? You're human. I can smell the weakness on you."

"So? Everybody knows the dragon around here. Please go." She shook her head, and her eyes pleaded. "Do not bring the dragon here."

Gunner glared at the man rolling around, groaning in pain and holding his snapped wrist. Gunner had been shot in the arm and he wasn't favoring it. All this guy had was a little broken bone. What a wuss.

"You want to kill him," Hallie said. "I can see it. You can't do that. If Damon doesn't get you, you'll be thrown in that damned shifter prison. Either option is bad."

Gunner narrowed his eyes. She was holding his gaze just fine right now, and the air was filled with a settled sensation of confidence. "I thought you were submissive."

"Sometimes I am, and sometimes I'm not." She jammed a finger at his bike. "If you don't leave now, I'll tase you again."

He believed her. Why? Because he could hear the truth in her voice. This woman might be submissive sometimes, but she didn't bluff.

Huh. Interesting.

Gunner backed away a few steps, and then sauntered off toward his motorcycle. The *pit-pat, pit-pat* of blood trickling down his hand was annoying, and made the air stink of wet pennies. That asshole had ruined his favorite hoodie.

He slid his leg over his bike and called out, "The tracker will be on your phone or on your car. Fix it." And then he turned his motorcycle on and peeled out of the gas station.

He looked back once, because he couldn't seem to help himself.

Hallie was standing there by that man's weapon, her eyes on Gunner, her phone up to her ear. She would be on the phone with the police now. At least there was that.

She gave him a little two-fingered wave, like she'd done in the gas station to Robby.

Gunner didn't wave back. He flipped his visor down and leaned down, hit the gears fast, and rocketed up the road.

That woman was something he didn't understand.

She'd been tough. She hadn't been nearly surprised enough to figure out her ex was tracking her. She'd asked Robby to delete the footage of Gunner throttling that man.

And for the most curious part...

When she'd asked him to leave, he had.

For him, his bear didn't get pulled off any prey, for any reason, but that little woman...that little human...could give him a little tase and tell him to leave, and all of a sudden his body was in his control?

Well, that didn't make any sense at all, now did it?

Gunner had been confused about himself before he'd pulled into that gas station, but now?

Now he was completely baffled.

TWO

Where was she?

Hallie fiddled with the curve of her hat brim and scanned the police station parking lot again. Corey had said she would be here.

A pair of headlights shone across her, and Hallie shielded her eyes. Corey's car pulled right up to the curb. Her cousin shoved the driver's side door open and ran to her. Hallie was already jogging down the steps, and caught her up in a crushing hug on the sidewalk.

"Shit, how did he find you?" Corey asked, holding her back at arm's length. "I thought you never talked about me to him."

"I don't know," Hallie whispered, shaking her

head.

She'd never seen her cousin look this worried—other than the night Hallie had shown up here four months ago, scared.

"Okay, where is your car?" Corey asked.

"It's parked over there, but I'm afraid he put a tracker in there or something. There was a man at the gas station. He said he would be tracking me using my phone or the car, but I checked my phone. He's not in there. One of the officers inside even helped me double-check it."

"You filed a harassment claim?" she asked.

"Y-yes. If something happens to me, I want them to have a good place to start looking."

"Nothing is going to happen to you. We should've come to the police from day one. I told you we should've."

"I thought he wouldn't find me here. I thought I would be safe."

Corey sighed and pulled her into a hug. "It's going to be okay. We're going to figure this out. What do you want to do with your car?"

"Leave it here."

"Forever?" Corey asked, her eyebrows drawing

down in confusion.

"Just until I can figure out where to take it to have it searched for a tracker."

"If there is a tracker in there, he will already know where we live."

Hallie shrugged. "I know. I just don't feel…"

"Feel what?"

"Safe."

"I hate him," Corey gritted out. "Hate his guts."

She wouldn't tell Corey what she was thinking now, but she was going to have to leave. Just the thought of it made her want to cry. These last four months with her cousin had been healing in so many ways, but she couldn't bring Derek's attention to Corey.

"Let's go home," Corey said. "I'll call a friend of mine in the morning. He's got a car shop. He might not know anything about trackers, but I bet he could point us in the right direction."

But just the thought of Corey involving anyone else gave Hallie a sinking feeling in her stomach.

Hallie got into the passenger's side of Corey's car and buckled in before she rolled her head back onto the rest behind her. She bit her lip to stop it from trembling. She'd been close to happiness here.

"What did the police say?" Corey asked softly.

"They can't do anything about the stalking until he does something bad to me."

"He has done bad to you," Corey gritted out as she pulled out of the parking lot. "Who was the guy who told you about the tracker? Can he check your car?"

"Oh, I don't even know his name. He was…" Hallie frowned. "He was shot."

"Oh my gosh!" Corey exclaimed. "Okay, back up, what the heck happened?"

"He's a shifter."

"From Damon's Mountains?" Okay, Corey sounded a little too excited for her own good.

"Yeah. This isn't leaving the car though. Pinky-promise me."

Hallie held out her pinky and Corey hooked hers with it. "I pinky-promise." Hallie knew she meant it because since they'd been kids, they had taken pinky-promises very seriously. Neither had ever broken a pinky-promise.

Hallie pulled her baseball cap lower onto her head and shoved her hands into the front pocket of her pink hoodie. "He asked to turn off the gas station cameras, and when Robby said no, he told him if Damon asks, it is who he thinks it is."

"Damon Daye?" Corey took her eyes off the road for too long, and Hallie had to point out a curb they were drifting toward. Corey yanked the car back between the lines. "The blue dragon. What did this guy look like?"

"He was riding a motorcycle—"

"Hot."

"Corey," she admonished. "He's probably somewhere digging a bullet out of his arm."

"If it was just in his arm, he's probably already fine. Those shifters heal freakily fast."

"Is freakily even a word?"

Corey shrugged. "Was he tall? Did he have muscles? Did he smell like an animal?"

"Oh my gosh, if you are just going to get re-interested in the shifter stuff, I'm not going to tell you any more. I'm tired."

"No, no, I'm asking for a reason! I swear."

Hallie glared at her, and then rested her head back again. "He wore a motorcycle helmet with one of those mirrored visors, but even that couldn't hide his glowing eyes. He said someone was following me. It was this tall guy in a black truck. Scar on his lip, dark eyes. I haven't seen him around here. He pulled him straight through the window. Just...one-handed, yanked him out. He hit him a couple times, and I thought the guy would die from the force. I've never seen anyone..." She swallowed hard. "I've never seen it happen to someone else. He was trying to control himself, I could tell. He was trying to be of service. Like...trying to help? The guy had a gun and he aimed it, and I was screaming, and he was shot in the arm. Look at this." She angled her body and showed Corey the front of her hoodie. There was a splatter of red across the chest. "That was fun to explain away to the police."

"You didn't tell them about the shifter?"

"No. He seemed..." Hallie shook her head and frowned, trying to put a finger on it. "He didn't care if he was hurt, or if Damon came for him. The growl in his chest was so loud and constant, and when he flipped his visor up, I could see his eyes."

"Hot?"

"Terrifying. One was silver, like mercury, and one was ice blue. Glowing like a demon's eyes. And they were...empty. I stopped him."

"Stopped him from what?"

"Killing that man."

"Why would you do that? If he wanted to get rid of your problem, you should've let him."

"I didn't want my stuff ruining someone else's life. Plus, that guy is just a product of one of my problems. If it wasn't him, Derek would send someone else. Killing him wouldn't solve anything. Maybe the police will be able to find him. They know his truck and the license plate now."

"What happened to the shifter?"

"He said to check my phone and my car for trackers, and then he rode away."

"Did he look back?" Corey asked.

Hallie cast a glance over at her. "Why?"

"Just curious."

"Yeah. He looked back once, and I waved, and he sped off on his bike. He had to be going one-fifty by the time he disappeared into the night."

"You met your first shifter," Corey said, turning onto Winding Creek Way.

"I've met shifters before."

"When we were kids. They had just been forced out into the public. Now, things are different."

"Different how?"

"If he's one of Damon's shifters, he will be registered."

Hallie's eyes flew wide, and her heart started pounding harder. "You think I should try to find him? Why?"

"Because if he knew about trackers in phones and in cars, he will probably know how to get rid of them."

The rest of the way up the mountain road to the family property that had been passed down to Corey, Hallie's mind raced a hundred miles a minute.

She'd thought about that shifter so much while she'd been waiting between police interviews. He'd protected her. Sure, he was gruff and growly, and borderline rude, but when it had come down to it, he had stuck up for her. She'd watched him break that man's wrist, pick up his gun, and pull all the pieces apart like he was military-trained or something. He'd dropped the pieces of the unusable gun onto the ground and picked that man up into the air with his bad arm. It would be burned into her mind for the rest of her life—that man with his helmet on, six-foot-five at least, visor up as he stared into that man's soul, backlit by the empty gas station. He'd done that for her.

"Well, perhaps I could bake him something as a thank-you, at the very least," she uttered quietly.

"Or…"

"Or what?"

"Empty out your life savings and offer to pay him for a bite."

"Corey!"

"What? Don't tell me you haven't thought about it."

"Thought about paying for a bite? You know they're only allowed one Turn. That one probably has a mate."

"I'm not saying to play housewife with him. All he has to do is bite you and move on with his life. You never even have to tell anyone."

"I would have to register! And I would have to link myself to my Maker! Why would I do any of that?"

"Because if Derek ever got the nuts to stop sending people to do his stalking for him, you could eat him alive." There was a steady grit to Corey's voice. She truly did hate Derek for the things he'd done.

Hallie let off a long exhale. "I'm not involving anyone else in my problems. And I definitely don't think turning into a mountain lion or a tiger or a crow or whatever that guy is will fix things for me. I'll figure something out."

"You can't run forever, Hallie."

A stubborn part of her whispered, *Watch me.* But the tired part of her agreed.

She would never ask for a bite, but she could bake him something and thank him for keeping her safe tonight. And then she would leave this place and figure out her next move.

Perhaps Derek wouldn't find her next hiding place.

THREE

Gunner canted his head and watched the red Subaru Outback pull out of the police station parking lot. He rocked back on his heels into the shadows as they passed.

She'd left her car in the parking lot, and had some woman pick her up. From the hug they'd exchanged, her friend had been through something big with her.

Good on Hallie for going to the police, but truth be told, he kind of wished she hadn't. He could get away with murder easier if there wasn't any ties to him and her stalker.

The problem with tonight—Hallie had garnered the attention of something far more dangerous than the man who was after her.

She'd perked up his inner grizzly.

And what a beautiful hunt this was.

He stood and strode for her car, careful to stay behind a row of taller vans to hide from the police cameras. He still wore his helmet. One check of the car door handle, and he shook his head. Hallie had left it unlocked. That woman had so much to learn, but also, if anyone wanted to get into her car or cause her harm, they would find a way.

Shifters could be monsters, but so could humans.

He sank into the car and pulled down the visor so it would shield his actions from the angle of the parking lot camera. When he did, a spare set of keys fell into his lap.

Tsk tsk tsk. Hallie, Hallie, Hallie. All the wrong moves.

A flash of a memory drifted across his mind. It was of the uncertainty and fear in her pretty hazel eyes as he had asked who would hate the shorts she was wearing.

A growl rippled from his chest as he ducked down and sniffed at the radio, the gear shift, and the passenger's seat. He would check the undercarriage of the car next, but he had a feeling he would find it inside.

Gunner ran his finger across a seam of carpet under the steering wheel that seemed out of place. He slid out of the car for a better angle and ripped the carpet down. There was a small circuit board, but the first plug-in looked different than the others. It had metal prongs, while the others were plastic.

He narrowed his eyes and pulled it out, replaced the carpet, and sat back in her car. Hmm. He'd been right, and that pretty woman was really being stalked more thoroughly than she'd even realized.

It made the blood in his veins boil.

He considered crushing it, but on second thought, he shoved it into his pocket. Let that motherfucker stalk *him* now. See where it got him—an early grave, likely.

Gunner retracted from the car. He locked the car and shut the door, then strode away from it, his back to the camera.

All it would pick up was black jeans, a destroyed black hoodie, and a motorcycle helmet.

Outside of that, he didn't care much about being caught. He didn't care about anything anymore.

Put him out of his fuckin' misery.

But this...this hunt...this mystery woman...she was a beautiful distraction from the hell he'd found himself in.

Gunner had ruined everything.

He'd fallen apart over the years, lost control of his animal, and then he'd done something even worse. He'd lost control of the man as well.

He'd burned his friends' lives to the ground.

He was a shifter with nothing to lose anymore, because his entire life had revolved around causing damage.

What a beautiful temptation to fix something for someone, for once, instead of destroying them.

He needed to find out who this tracker belonged to.

Gunner jogged across the street and into the dark lot a block away, then slid his leg over the seat of his motorcycle and turned the key. The engine growled to life.

He needed to see someone he trusted to figure out this tracking device.

Someone who understood technology, but was quiet about it.

Someone who had been around since he'd been

born.

He needed to return to Damon's Mountains and visit Bash of the Boarlanders.

FOUR

It was four in the morning, and Hallie still couldn't sleep.

She couldn't keep her eyes off the slow-spinning ceiling fan above her, illuminated by the glow of a small, plug-in nightlight. She'd never been scared of the dark until the last year, and now she had to have some kind of light to be able to let her body go vulnerable with unconsciousness. Usually when she couldn't sleep like this, it was because she had that scared, hunted feeling from what she'd been through, but tonight her mind was spinning round and round like the ceiling fan above her for a different reason.

She couldn't stop thinking about the shifter in the motorcycle helmet.

She'd worn herself out last night trying to track down all the registrants of Damon's Mountains, and she'd found a name for a shifter with bi-colored eyes that had most recently belonged to the newly-created Warlander Crew. The website offered a pitifully small amount of information though. Just his name, his height, an estranged brother, his parents—Haydan and Cassie of the Ashe Crew—and that he had bi-colored eyes. And that he was a grizzly shifter. Nothing more.

A grizzly shifter. Geez. She'd seen some of those Changing on the news when she was a little girl. The Keller brothers, Fire Bears of a crew of firefighters, had gone wild in their town and it had created a snowball effect that pushed shifters into the public eye, with them eventually being required to register.

Grizzly shifter. Shhhhit. Those were terrifying.

She'd been scared of shifters when she was younger. The news was brutal on them, and any mistake they made was hashed out in the public eye. They were discriminated against, and sure, even Hallie had bought into the negative media attention back when she was younger. Now? Oh, she believed they were dangerous, but they also had protective instincts, and one had used those for her benefit.

All his registration information did was whet her appetite for more information on the mystery shifter.

Her phone lit up on her bedside table, and an awful feeling took her gut. It would be Derek. He would've tracked down her new number and it would be some threatening, terrifying, vile message.

But when she propped up on her elbow and looked at the glowing phone screen, it was a message from Corey, who was supposed to be sleeping in the next room.

It was a link to some website called Bangaboarlander.com.

Hallie pulled her reading glasses on and poked the link.

Gunner Walker
Age: 35
Unmated, unpaired
Recently let go from the Warlander Crew
Lone grizzly
No current Crew
Grizzly shifter
Dangerous

Not suitable for pairing at this time.

Not suitable for pairing at this time.

She read that part a few times before she relaxed back in bed and messaged Corey. *How did you find this?* Send.

I used to troll this website back when I was over men, fantasizing about fucking a shifter instead.

Hallie snorted. Well, at least Corey owned her stuff.

He sounds like a mess. Send.

Just like someone else I know. See you in a few hours. Night cuz.

Cuz was what they'd always called each other since they were little. Hallie couldn't help the smile that confiscated her lips. They were cousins, but their moms had been so close, most of the time Corey felt like a sister.

Night cuz. Send.

Hallie settled the phone onto her chest and watched the fan. There was a 'message about this shifter' button at the bottom of Gunner's page.

Gunner Walker.

Such a cool name for a badass man.

Not suitable for pairing at this time.

Same.

She huffed a laugh and shook her head. Hallie would never be okay to pair up either, because she would never trust a man ever again.

Men lied.

They said pretty words and got women hooked, and then they hurt them, manipulated them, took over their minds, and trained them to protect secrets that hurt.

Hallie squeezed her eyes closed at a wave of memories that took over her mind.

She was probably a bigger mess than Gunner.

Not suitable.

Not suitable.

Hallie inhaled deeply and lifted her phone back up. She hit the message button, and typed out:

Hello, to whomever this concerns.

Gunner showed me a kindness tonight. I'm not interested in pairing either, just in finding out how I can contact him. I would like to thank him for what he went out of his way to do for me. It was nice to feel like someone had my back.

She typed out her phone number and email address, but hesitated before she hit send.

I will be at the Korner Katch Bar and Grill tonight at 8:00 p.m., straight after I get off work. I will bring cookies as a thank-you. I'm not good at much, but I can bake. See him there, or not. Either way, I hope he knows there is someone out in this world that appreciates what he did.

She signed her name, and then before she could change her mind, she hit send.

FIVE

Gunner lifted his hand to knock, then hesitated, twisted around, and glared at the gray streaks in the sky. It was six in the morning and before dawn. It was too early to be here.

He should leave.

He made a clicking sound behind his teeth, then jogged down the stairs and made his way to his motorcycle. This was stupid.

But...Bash could find out who this tracker was connected to. He could find out anything.

Gunner turned and headed for the porch of Bash Kane, then turned again and gripped his hair in his hands. He glared at the dark sky, where the last of the stars twinkled their goodbyes to the night.

When he looked at his motorcycle, someone was standing at the edge of the woods.

He recognized the silhouette and scent immediately.

"I thought you would be long gone," Lucia Novak, the daughter of Beaston Novak, said.

Her raven-dark hair lifted in the breeze, and her bright-green eyes remained trained on him.

Chills lifted on his forearms.

Lucia was very important to these mountains. She was a seer, like her father.

She was also the reason he was walking free.

"How did you know I was here?" he asked.

"I had a dream about you."

"Just now?"

She nodded. "And the night before. And the night before that. I dreamed you were going to walk away from what you needed to do."

Gunner inhaled deeply and frowned at the trailer Bash shared with his mate, Emerson. "I should've left. I meant to, but I just got stuck."

Lucia gave him a slow smile that he didn't understand. "Do you know I've seen what happens to you?" she asked. Chills, chills, chills. She sauntered a few steps closer. "You're going to be okay."

He laughed. He couldn't help himself. "You don't know me at all then."

"I know you better than you think."

"Everyone hates me."

"Everyone, who?"

"The Warlanders."

"They're disappointed. They're sad. They're angry. If they hated you, they would think nothing of you." She twitched her chin toward Bash's single-wide trailer in Boarland Mobile Park. "You're going to open a door that changes things. Or…" She arched a dark eyebrow. "You're going to ignore your destiny and walk away, like you do in my dreams."

Gunner cracked his knuckles. "If it happens in your vision, why should I fight what's going to happen?"

"Because that's what you're good at. Fighting everything."

"Why did you let me out of that cage?" he asked. He'd wondered that since the night he'd set the Warlander's mobile homes on fire. Lucia had come to the cage he'd been drawn into, and she had opened it and set him free.

Lucia smiled. "Because I've seen what you can do."

"Destroy?"

"Yes," she murmured. "But there are two kinds of destruction. Destruction for bad, and destruction for good. Prove me right, Gunner. Prove that my faith in you isn't wasted."

Gunner dropped his gaze to the grass at his feet. He had to. He didn't want Lucia to see the emotion in his gaze. She was perhaps the only person who believed in him like that, but didn't she see? Didn't she understand? His destiny was to destroy for bad.

"Ask him," Lucia said as she walked back into the shadows of the woods. With her back to him, she said, "If you don't try, then how will you ever know what you are capable of?"

Gunner dug in his pocket and held up the tracker to ask if she had seen it in her visions, but Lucia had disappeared into the trees as if she had never existed at all. He was alone in the clearing, holding up the tracker.

"What is that?" a deep, sleep-filled voice asked from behind him.

Startled, Gunner spun and crouched, a snarl in his

throat.

Sebastian Kane stood on the porch of his single-wide trailer—tall, strong, dark-haired, glowing green eyes reflecting like an animal's in the dim light of his porch.

Gunner slowly stood and stifled the snarl in his chest. Bash had never meant anyone any harm. "It's a tracker, I think."

"Mmm. Come on inside. Something needs to be seen."

"Something needs to be seen?" he asked, confused on how he'd worded it.

"Yes. By you."

Bash turned and disappeared inside. The click of the closing screen door sounded loud out here in the dark before dawn.

Gunner took the stairs and entered slowly. Smelled like dominant grizzly in here. Sometimes his animal posted up in small spaces, but this morning he seemed to be quiet and contained.

Bash was standing in the kitchen with his back to Gunner. "Don't want to fight you."

"I'm not fighting."

"Then why are you always growling?"

Gunner rolled his eyes closed and tried to stifle it. Didn't work. "It's just how I am now."

"Your dad is worried. Your mom is beside herself. You haven't called them enough."

"I just need space from everything."

Bash was making coffee, but twitched his head at the table. A piece of paper laid crooked on the round four-seater.

With a frown, Gunner approached it slowly, then lifted the paper up to read it in the dim light.

Hello, to whomever this concerns.

Gunner showed me a kindness tonight. I'm not interested in pairing either, just in finding out how I can contact him. I would like to thank him for what he went out of his way to do for me. It was nice to feel like someone had my back.

There was a phone number and an email address. Hallielynn69. Ha.

I will be at the Korner Katch Bar and Grill tonight at 8:00 p.m., straight after I get off work. I will bring cookies as a thank-you. I'm not good at much, but I can bake. See him there, or not. Either way, I hope he knows there is someone out in this world that appreciates what he did.

"When did this come through?" Gunner asked.

"I can hear how fast your heart is beating," Bash said as he brought two mugs of coffee to the table. He set one in front of Gunner, took a seat across the table, and took a careful sip of his steaming beverage. "It came through a couple hours ago."

So…what could that mean. She was up all night thinking about sending this? How had she tracked him down? How had she figured out the Bangaboarlander site? She was human. Humans weren't supposed to know about it.

He read up to his description but stopped at the final line of his page. *Not suitable for pairing at this time.*

"I don't need this information," he murmured as he folded the paper in half.

"You already memorized that number, and her email, and where she will be tonight." Bash pointed to his face. "Your pupils dilated when you read that information."

"You pay too much attention to things that don't matter."

"Mmm. I've been told that before."

"By who?"

"Assface Clinton."

Gunner snorted and a grin took his face for a second before he could compose it again. Clinton and Bash went at it sometimes, but then, Clinton picked battles with everyone at some point. Like his damn son, Landon.

A piercing pain took his chest as he thought about Lucia's mate. Gunner had hurt them all.

It's all he knew how to do.

Not suitable for pairing...ever.

"I was scared too," Bash said.

Gunner shoved the folded paper into the middle of the table. "Scared of what?"

"Emerson."

"I'm not scared of anyone," Gunner gritted out. He lifted the tracker and set it on the table with a soft click. "Can you find out who this belongs to?"

Bash narrowed his eyes at it. "If they paid for it with credit card."

"I need a name and an address."

"You hunting?"

Gunner tipped his coffee back and embraced the

scorching burn as the liquid seared down the back of his throat. He chugged it down to the last drop, and stood. "The hunt is the only thing that makes sense anymore."

"Mmm," Bash said. He made that noise a lot, and for some reason, it annoyed Gunner.

"What?" he asked.

"You got an anger in you, boy. You remind me of your dad when he was your age. He can tell you stories about anger. So can your momma."

"Why are you telling me this?"

"Because sometimes it's nice to be wrong."

"Wrong about what?" he gritted out, growing frustrated with riddle-time.

"Wrong about being alone."

Well, that halted the anger. Gunner forced himself to look away from Bash's steady green gaze. Bash had always been a watcher.

Bash leaned forward, reaching, and gently plucked the tracker from the table. "I'll call you as soon as I know if I can find him or not."

"Appreciate it. I can pay."

Bash snorted and shook his head. "You want to pay? I take favors."

"What favor?"

"Call your momma and let her know you're still alive."

Gunner huffed a sigh, then nodded once. "See you when I see you, Bash."

"Korner Katch, eight p.m.," Bash called as Gunner left his house.

Gunner rolled his eyes and scanned the woods for Lucia, but he didn't sense anything out there anymore besides the little forest creatures who were too dumb to realize they were shacking up in the territory of the Boarlanders.

Gunner sauntered to his motorcycle at the edge of the trees, but movement caught his attention. A massive silverback walked slowly on all fours at the edge of the trees. Kirk, Lucas's father, stopped and slammed a fist against the earth in warning.

Gunner picked his helmet off his motorcycle, pulled it over his head, and buckled it under his chin as he held Kirk's gaze. Of course he was angry with him. He'd burned Lucas's trailer park. The slamming of a screen door sounded, and now Clinton was standing on the porch of his trailer—chin high in the air, blazing silver eyes boring into Gunner.

Any other day, he would've welcomed the fight, but right now he was existing under the weight of what he'd done. Of course Landon and Lucas's families were angry.

He deserved their hate.

He slid his leg over the seat and started his bike, then peeled out, spewing gravel. The rule with dominants was never to give your back to them. It encouraged their animal instincts to chase him, but right about now Gunner didn't care about living or dying. If Kirk and Clinton chased him down, he deserved it. He would do his best to keep his grizzly in check to give them a chance.

I've seen what you can do.

Lucia's voice whispered through his mind. He shifted up and hit the accelerator, desperate to rid himself of the voices.

He knew what he could do too, and it was bad news for everyone.

SIX

Hallie checked the time on her phone again.

He hadn't showed.

She checked her email again, but there was nothing new there. It was half past eight, and she felt so stupid sitting here at a table by herself in a crowded bar with a plate of cookies. There was an older couple at a nearby table that kept looking over at her with pity in their eyes. She must've looked so pathetic. She'd been sitting here for half an hour, just sipping on a soda water and waiting for a stranger.

Her phone lit up with a text, and silly hope bloomed in her chest as she fumbled to hold up the phone to see the screen. It was a message from Corey. *I'm outside whenever you are ready.*

Dejected, Hallie shoved her phone into her purse and laughed at herself. He probably hadn't even seen her message to the Bangaboarlander website, but she had been thinking over it all day at work. She'd even rushed home and gotten all gussied up for this meetup that she'd completely constructed in her mind.

"This is so dumb," she whispered as she set a five-dollar bill on the table for the soda water.

"You deserve better," the sweet lady at the next table told her as she passed.

Hallie gripped the plate of cookies tighter and tried to smile. "Thanks. You guys have a good night."

She didn't deserve better. She didn't deserve anything from that man. He had already put himself at risk to protect her, and he didn't know her at all. Hallie didn't feel like explaining that to the nice couple though, so she just walked out of the bar without a single look back.

Outside, she checked the parking lot to make sure there was no one paying too much attention. Back to feeling scared everywhere she went. Derek knew where she was, so the happiness she had found here in Laramie was snuffed out.

Corey was parked at the back of the lot. She flashed her lights a couple of times, then shrugged up her hands in question.

Hallie shook her head. He hadn't come.

"Maybe he didn't get the message," Corey said as she got inside the car.

"Or maybe he isn't interested in revisiting last night's weirdness. It's okay. More cookies for us."

Corey was staring with a pity that matched the nice couple in the bar.

"I'm fine. I don't care. I just wanted to say thank you."

Corey nodded and pulled out of the parking lot, and as they hit the main road, Hallie watched the buildings of the small town square blur by until Corey slowed. "Uuuuh, Hallie?" she asked softly.

Startled, Hallie looked around just in time to see a familiar all-black motorcycle settle right beside Corey's door at the red light. The rider was dressed in black jeans, a black T-shirt, black riding gloves, and the helmet with the mirrored gold visor she'd memorized from last night. He was looking straight ahead, but angled his head slowly and stared for a three-count before he twitched his head in a come-here motion.

"This is the hottest thing I've ever been a part of, and it's not even about me," Corey whispered.

"I can't go out there."

"Why not?"

"The light is about to turn green!"

"I don't think he gives a shit about stopping traffic," Corey argued.

"Right." Hallie shoved her door open and gripped the cookies, jogged around the back of the car, and came to a stop beside him. "Hi."

Gunner's helmet tilted down to the cookies and then back to her, but he didn't say anything.

"I tried to message you, and then I went to a bar and I thought you might show up, so I made these." She shoved the cookies at him. "They're for you. To thank you. For you know…taking a bullet for me."

He just stared.

The light turned green.

Someone behind Corey honked, and she rolled down her window. "Fuck off!"

Gunner straightened up, his boots on the ground to steady the motorcycle. He unfastened the helmet, then slid it off his head. This was the first time she'd seen his face in full, and oh...my...goodness.

She'd never seen a more striking man in all her life.

He had some faint scarring on the right side of his hairline, and he had dark whiskers from a couple days' growth. His face was chiseled, his lips masculine, and his eyes...well, his eyes captured her completely.

They really were two colors. She hadn't imagined it last night after all.

One was churning silver, and one was blue.

He took a cookie, shoved the entire thing into his mouth, and then pulled his helmet over her head. She was temporarily blinded by both shock and the helmet blocking her vision of the world, but he got it settled over her fast enough.

The cookies disappeared from her hands. She turned to see Corey holding up her phone, filming her, with a big grin on her face and the plate of cookies in her other hand.

"Have fun, use a condom," Corey said.

Another honk sounded, and Corey turned. "I will fucking fight you!" She transformed her face back into a smile and nodded at Hallie. "Have fun, make good decisions. But not too good. Make a story you can tell your kids someday. Okay then, bye-bye now."

When she turned back to the mystery man, Gunner was pushing down a peg on the bike. "Get on," he told her.

"But...what do I do with these?" she asked about her cross-body purse and the phone in her hand.

A growl rumbled from him. She parted her lips to apologize, but he pulled the purse over her head, unclipped the strap from both clips, and clicked them expertly to two of her belt loops. He tossed the strap, and Corey caught it. "I used to play softball," she said proudly after catching it. "Co-ed, freshman year in college. I was second base."

Hallie pursed her lips against a smile at the excitement in Corey's voice. Gunner took her phone from her grasp, shoved it down the front of her tank top, and secured it into her bra. She didn't know why, but that smooth move made her nethers all tingly.

He held out a hand, and this was her last chance to bail. He was a stranger. Not suitable. Terrifying. Strong. Aggressive and violent. But he'd used it for good, and for some reason, she really wanted to go with him.

"I've never done this," she whispered breathlessly as she slid her hand against his.

His grasp was shockingly strong as he helped her swing a leg over the back of his motorcycle. "Boots on the pegs, hold onto my waist, don't fall off."

Right. Don't fall off. She scooted closer to his back and slid her arms around his waist, and then squeaked as he took off through the stale yellow light.

Corey was cheering like a maniac behind them, and Hallie would've laughed if her lungs weren't somewhere on the pavement behind them. Too fast, too fast, too fast!

The wind whipped at her skin, and she squeezed her eyes tightly closed as the town blurred by.

This was what it felt like to be a bullet.

He jerked slightly every time he changed gears, and they flew faster and faster until she couldn't catch her breath. She clung to him for dear life until at last, he slowed.

After a few breathless moments, she dared to open her eyes, but she had no idea where they were. She gingerly sat up and twisted just enough to see the lights of Laramie far behind them.

"That was terrifying!"

"You feel alive though."

"Half alive! I thought I was going to fall off!"

"Well, now you can enjoy the ride."

"What about 'I've never done this before' did you not understand?"

"All of it. Best way to get you to loosen up is to get you desensitized straight out of the gate," he called over the whipping wind.

"Don't you need this helmet?" she asked, concerned. "That was really dangerous."

"I would survive a crash. You wouldn't."

She frowned at his back, then dared to release her death grip on his waist and lifted the sleeve of his black T-shirt up. She could see the exit wound from the bullet he'd been shot with last night. It was red and angry, but it looked half-healed already.

It hit her in that moment how different they were. He really wasn't human.

When she looked up, she caught him looking at her in the side-view mirror with a look of confusion swirling in his glowing eyes. "It doesn't hurt."

Hallie swallowed hard. "I'm glad," she called over the wind. "I was a little worried."

Gunner shook his head, but he didn't say anything

else, and now it was hard for her to keep her gaze off the side-view mirror and those glowing bi-colored eyes of his. If the wind bothered him, he didn't show it.

They were quiet for a long time after that, and she relaxed into the cadence of the ride and the sway of the road through the mountains. It was summertime, but the wind drew gooseflesh from her bare arms. The tank top had been a good decision for a bar, but not for a ride.

"Where are we going?" she asked.

"You nervous?"

"That you're a stalker? Take a number, get in line," she deadpanned. She thought she saw a flash of a smile in the mirror, but it was gone just as soon as it appeared.

He slowed and seemed to be looking for something in the dark. There were no streetlights out here, so she was surprised when he turned off on a single-lane dirt road.

"Hold on," he told her as they climbed steadily up and up, up the winding dirt road. Gunner didn't so much as spin out his back tire the entire ride up. When he finally came to a stop beside a huge machine, she was so confused.

"What is this?" she asked as he offered his hand to help her get off.

"An old worksite."

She got off and wrung her hands as she looked around. It was so dark out here, and the half-moon wasn't giving enough light. "Am I...am I safe?" she asked nervously.

She'd really gotten on the back of a motorcycle with a stranger and let him take her deep into the mountains.

"Pull your phone out and drop your location to your friend," he said as he got off the bike and rested it on its kickstand.

He pulled his gloves off, set them on the seat, and then strode for the huge machine that sat on the edge of the steep mountainside.

"Right." Surely he was safe if he was telling her to give Corey her location.

"She's my cousin," Hallie called. "Not just my friend. Her name is Corey."

"Ask her for the video of us leaving," he called from somewhere in the dark.

"Is that why you blasted out of there? For the

video?"

He didn't answer, but that was okay. She was busy dropping a location pin to Corey just in case.

Bright side, the reception out here was fantastic.

"Here," he said out of nowhere.

She yelped and startled hard, but he was just holding out a hoodie.

"You look cold. I heard humans are fragile."

She took the hoodie and considered arguing, but she remembered how he'd smiled after he'd been shot. Yep, compared to him, she was freaking fragile.

She pulled on the giant hoodie, and the hem fell to her knees. Adorable.

She laughed and jogged to catch up to him, stumbled, and barely caught herself. He sat down on a bench and gestured for her to sit at the other end of it. She sat in the middle of the bench, but he shooed her farther away.

"What, no cuddling?" she teased.

An annoyed flash of those glowing eyes told her he wasn't amused.

"I don't cuddle, and this isn't like that."

"Not suitable for pairing," she recited. "You and me both, buddy."

"Buddy," he growled.

She heaved a sigh and cuddled into the oversized hoodie, drew her knees up to her chest, and looked over the edge of the steep mountainside. There had to be a hundred felled trees here. "You're a logger?"

"I was. Now I don't know what I am."

"Did you get fired?"

"Yep."

"Oh." She frowned. "I'm sorry."

"No one to blame but me."

"What happened?"

"Derek Forester, two-nine-nine-three-five River Canyon Road, Kansas City, Kansas."

She froze, and chills lifted the hair on the back of her neck. "How did you find that out?"

"I found the tracker in your car. You can drive it now. It's safe."

"You…you broke into my car."

"Can't break into an unlocked car, Hallie. Be more careful."

She crossed her arms over her chest and stared out into the valley below. "Derek is dangerous—"

"I am dangerous."

She remembered the way he'd held that man up

with one hand last night, and any argument she'd had got lost in her throat.

"I'll figure it out."

He slid her a glance, and then went back to staring down the hill. "I don't have control of my animal. I used to be foreman here. I had a three-man crew under me, but I couldn't control my temper." He twitched his head toward the huge machine. "That's new. I rolled the last one down the hill and almost killed my work crew. There were two humans in it."

"Two humans," she whispered. "And the third was a shifter?"

Gunner nodded. "He was one of my Crewmates."

"In the Warlanders?"

He frowned over at her. "How did you know?"

"It's on your registration."

An empty smile took his lips. "So I hunted Derek, and you hunted me?"

"We're both a mess," she quipped unapologetically.

"I just told you I rolled a machine down the hill while I was going after my crew, and got fired from my job, and you think your mess is comparable to mine?"

Hallie shrugged. "I can say I have no interest in competing over who has the biggest shit-show of a life. But…" She rolled her head over so she could see his profile when she said, "I've been on the run for twelve months, and am no closer to fixing my problems than I was the day I left. I can't have friends or settle into a job. Closest I've gotten is in Laramie, with Corey."

"Your cousin."

"Yes, my cousin."

"She's the reason you came here?" he asked.

"Yep. I never told Derek about her, or how close we were as kids. I thought I could maybe be safe here."

"You are safe here." He said it so off the cuff and confident.

God, she wished she could believe it. "You have no idea how beautiful that sounds."

"He hurt you?" he asked, and she didn't miss the growl in his voice.

She shrugged up one shoulder. "It was another life."

"What happened to your nose?" he asked.

A flush of heat took her cheeks, and she looked

away as anger consumed her. "Too deep," she muttered.

"Too deep, too fast. You're leaving soon, aren't you?" he asked.

"Yes."

"Then what does it matter? I'll be leaving soon too. Who will I tell? I don't talk to anyone."

Hallie wrapped her arms around her legs, rested her cheek on her knees, and watched him. "No one at all?"

He shook his head.

"What about your brother?"

"Captain? Chh. I haven't talked to him in years. I don't even think about him. Ever. We split ways a long time ago."

"That's sad. What about your parents? They are still alive. They're in the Ashe Crew. Or what about the Warlanders?"

He inhaled deeply, and she could see the shutdown on his face. "Too deep."

Oooooh. They were both messes.

"He broke my nose, and then he wouldn't let me go to the doctor to fix it. He said he wanted me to be reminded every time I looked in the mirror."

"Reminded of what?" he said in a voice too deep and gritty to be human.

"To never talk back."

Gunner let off an empty laugh that filled the clearing. "I'm going to kill him someday." There was a promise in his voice.

Chills rippled up her spine again. He sounded so sure of himself. She believed him, and she didn't know what terrified her more—the fact that she wasn't running, or the fact that she wanted him to.

Mess, mess, mess.

"He'll get tired of chasing me eventually. He will find someone else to manipulate."

"Why you?"

She shrugged. "I ask myself that a lot. I'm nothing special." She didn't say more.

"How soon are you leaving?"

"Tomorrow."

"Jesus. Does Corey know?"

"No. I don't do goodbyes. I'm kind of weak about them."

He stared at her for a while. "I can hear when you tell the truth."

She puffed air out of her cheeks. "I wish I had that

ability. I have terrible taste in men. I could've avoided all of this if I could've just heard the lies."

"It's refreshing," Gunner said.

She didn't understand. "Refreshing knowing someone has terrible taste in—"

"I mean the honesty is refreshing. You don't care about the show."

"What show?"

"Putting on your best face to make someone like you."

She puffed out a big sigh. "I have been humbled a thousand times, and I am swimming around rock bottom, Gunner. Plus, I tased you within five minutes of meeting you. If you like my company, that would be nice, but if not, I don't cry over much anymore."

"And that's the refreshing part. You own your shit. Makes it easy for people around you to own their shit."

"You want to do a confession?" she asked, starting to understand.

"Chhh." He relaxed back onto the bench, stared at the felled trees below, and draped his arm across the back of the seat. His fingertips almost reached her shoulder.

"You ever hit a woman?" she asked.

The look of absolute disgust on his face was answer enough.

"You ever hunted a woman?" she asked.

He twitched his head no.

"Hurt any kids?"

"Fuck no, and never would."

"Then you're fine by me."

Gunner leaned forward and rested his elbows on his knees, narrowed eyes trained on her as he cracked his knuckles. "I set all my Crew's houses on fire."

"Did they deserve it?"

"No. They're good people."

"Why did you do it?"

"Because it's what I do. I destroy the things I care about."

"You do it, or your animal does it?"

"What's the difference? It's still me."

"A man who doesn't have control of his animal is different than a man not being in control of the man."

"What's your deal?" he asked angrily, standing.

She was confused, so she didn't answer. She just waited as he paced away and knelt down near the edge of the ridge. He stood, and seemed agitated as he ran his hands through his hair. "What happened to you that you can sit there with a steady voice and say terrible things are okay?"

She shook her head, still not understanding.

"If a man tells you the terrible things he's done, you should punish him."

"Is that..." She swallowed hard. "Is that what you need? Punishment?"

Ooooh, the vulnerability in his eyes ripped at her heart.

"Wait," she said as he strode away. "Do you want me to insult you?"

"No! I want you to call it as you see it. Stop with this nice-girl shit. If I tell you something evil I've done, tell me I'm fucking evil!"

He walked toward the machine, talking low to himself.

Oh, she recognized this. Guilt did awful things to people sometimes, and this was a man being eaten alive by it.

She stood and slowly followed him. "Gunner?"

He paced back toward her and then away, still talking to himself.

"Gunner?" she asked again.

"What?" he growled.

"I..."

"You what?"

"I go to therapy."

He straightened up and looked as surprised as she was by her admission.

"I haven't even told Corey I've been going. I go at three on Tuesdays and Thursdays to this little building on Main Street, and then I sit in the parking lot and I try to cry, but I never can. Then I drive down to this little bar three blocks away. I go in and have a shot of whiskey, and I think over everything I'm learning about myself, and one of those things is that I'm bombproof."

His chest was heaving with his breath. "Bombproof," he repeated.

"I don't react to big things anymore because I've been through some stuff that desensitized me to...well, to everything. If you want me to throw insults at you, you have to give me some kind of signal. Otherwise, you won't find any judgement from me. Who am I to judge? My life is a fucking disaster, and I am a participant. I'm not just a victim, Gunner. I make bad decisions."

Hands on his hips, he just stared at her in silence. At last he said, "I also make bad decisions."

She pursed her lips against a smile and twirled the too-long sleeves of the hoodie around her wrists, and then twirled them the other way. "Want to make bad decisions together?"

"Like what?"

She pointed to the big machine. "We could make out in that tractor."

"It's not a tractor, and also you shouldn't want to make out with someone who just admitted they burned their Crew's houses."

"Well…did you tell them you are sorry?"

He chewed on the corner of his lip, and then shook his head. "I haven't talked to them."

"My therapist would probably tell you that for closure, you should say your apologies."

"I don't like what you're doing."

"What am I doing?" she asked.

"You're making things clear," he growled, waving his hand near his temple. "I don't like change."

"Can't just keep going like you're going."

"Yes, I absolutely can."

"Fine. Do it."

He lifted his frustrated gaze to her. "I need to think."

"Why did you bring me here?" she asked suddenly.

He glanced around. "Because I couldn't do the bar you wanted to meet at. Too many people, and I don't trust anyone."

"Don't trust anyone, or don't trust yourself?"

"Stop!"

"Stop what?"

"Seeing me!"

A fluttering sensation filled her middle as she dropped her gaze. "Thank you."

"For what?" he asked, pacing back and forth.

"For helping me last night."

He gave her his back, linked his hands behind his head, and struggled to suck in breath, and she recognized that.

He dragged more air into his lungs, but it was a short breath. It was panic.

She padded over to him and rested her hand on the small of his back. "Shhhhhh."

He drew his elbows in and tried for another

breath. "If I Change, don't run. Just be still."

"I'm not ready for you to Change in front of me."

He didn't answer.

"Hey," she whispered, stepping around him. She dragged her light touch around his waist and looked up at him. "Hey," she repeated softer. "Look at me."

He tried and failed to drag air into his lungs again, and she could hear it—the growl that rattled up his chest.

"I'm not ready to see that, and you're not ready to show me that. Please stay."

"Please stay," he repeated, but his voice was unrecognizable now.

"Stay. Keep me safe."

He inhaled, and it was a longer breath this time.

She smiled and nodded up at him. "Keep me safe," she repeated, because she could see the effect those words had on him.

Gunner wasn't evil.

He was injured. He was hurt. Damaged.

Damaged could recognize damaged.

"I take it back," he murmured. "I don't want you to call me out anymore."

She huffed a soft laugh and dared to lean forward,

rested her forehead on his chest. She could feel how hard and fast his heart was pounding. Hers was racing too. He felt so heavy. Even the air was hard to breathe this close to him right now.

"No more callouts. We can talk about what we like on our hot dogs for all I care. No more *deep* tonight, okay?"

He stunned her by slipping his hand behind her head and holding her there against his chest. He massaged her gently, gripped the back of her hair, then released her. "No more deep," he agreed, and eased back.

"Are you really leaving tomorrow?" he asked.

She nodded. "I've already packed."

He cocked his head and searched her eyes. "I've been trying to leave for weeks."

"Why don't you?"

"The bear has territory set up. He won't leave it."

"Ever?" she asked.

He shook his head. "I'm stuck."

She inhaled deeply and looked over the edge of the ledge where he used to work. He'd set fire to his old life, and what a suffocating feeling to be stuck like this in the chaos he created. Maybe it was just.

Perhaps it was fair, but she felt for him. She wished it was different.

She straightened her spine, and couldn't believe she was about to say what she was thinking.

"My offer stands."

"Offer," he repeated softly.

"I've never had a one-night stand. I'm feeling reckless. I've never been this transparent with anyone in my entire life. I'm on birth control. There will be no strings attached. I won't ask for more than you can give. I won't need attention afterward."

He lifted his chin higher into the air. "What's in it for you then?"

"You can make me forget everything for a little while, can't you?"

There were three breaths—each staring at the other, lost in consideration—before Gunner slid his big, strong hand around hers and led her toward the big machine.

She had a moment of panic as her brain caught up to what she'd done. She'd asked for a one-night stand that wouldn't mean anything past tonight. She'd asked a stranger to quiet her mind from the stupid flashbacks that had been tickling her mind since he'd pointed out her broken nose.

She'd asked for an escape, and he was going to give it to her.

Her dark hero.

He climbed up onto the track of the huge machine, opened the door, helped her up inside, and scooted the seat back as far as it would go as she slid her leg over his and straddled his lap.

"First one-night stand," he murmured, searching her eyes.

"Yes. Be gentle."

He slid his hand around her throat, and she tilted her chin back and smiled down at him. His wicked grin met hers. "You want it gentle? You sure?"

"I want it however you think I need it."

"Oooh, little human," he rumbled next to her ear as he pulled her in by her throat. "All you have to do is exist now. I'll make you forget it all."

Hallie rolled her eyes closed at how good that sounded. His lips pressed to her neck and she scooted up, rested right against his cock—swollen and hard against the seam of his jeans. Biting her lip, she eased back and pulled his shirt up and over his head. He was all muscle, and a crisscross of scars across his torso that said he was comfortable with war. She ran her hands through his hair and he arched his head back, exposing his Adam's apple to her kiss. He rolled his hips as he gripped hers and pulled her against him.

He was smooth with how he slid his hands up her shirt and peeled the hoodie and tank top off as one. All that remained was the black lace bra she'd thrown on before she went to that bar in hopes of getting to talk to him again. His body moved like water against hers as he sat up straighter and pulled her tight against him. His pounding heartbeat went straight through her, and she reveled in the fact that she could affect a man like him.

She'd never felt more beautiful than in this moment in the dim moonlight, with a man in a moment that no one else would ever have to know about.

In this world, they were the only ones who existed.

She moved with him as his hands dragged her this way and that, massaging her, exploring her skin.

The snap of her bra dragged shivers up her spine, and that first feel of his strong hands cupping her bare breasts made her inhale sharply and close her eyes to the world.

She surrendered.

She didn't remember how he got her jeans off. She didn't remember unzipping his jeans. It was as if she was caught underwater in a strong current and was at the whim of the ocean. She straddled his lap again, not a stitch of clothing to shield her, and felt the stone width of his cock against her sex. This was everything.

He was huge, but it didn't scare her. Nothing about him did. Not in this moment.

She rolled her hips, pressing her wet sex against his shaft, and the grunt of pleasure that emanated from him drew another wave of shivers up her spine. His hands were strong on her back, on the side of her neck, and it was in this moment that he angled his chin up and pressed his lips to hers for the first time.

She could taste the electricity. She straightened and rolled against him, pressed her breasts to his chest just to feel the strength there, and kissed him back.

She'd never had such immediate chemistry with anyone, ever.

What they were doing, this dance, it was magic.

He pressed his tongue gently past her lips, and she got to taste him for the first time. This connection was everything, and she'd been right—he was making her forget everything.

Gunner shoved his jeans farther down his thighs and gripped her outer legs, dragged her against him. The head of his cock teased her entrance and she angled slightly to take him, but Gunner was preparing her. She could tell he cared about not hurting her.

He was taking his time, getting her wetter, making sure she could take him.

Bad boy, but a good man.

His smell was intoxicating. It was a mixture of cologne and animal, and made her senses swim. He gripped her legs and dragged her up his cock again, and now it was so slick, the friction made her feel good. She gasped and rolled her hips again, desperate to take him.

"You gonna be a good girl?" he asked. "You gonna take all of me?"

"Yes," she whispered shakily. "Please."

A soft growl rumbled from his chest, and she rolled her eyes closed and melted into him. She loved that sexy sound. Gunner was dragging her up and down his swollen cock, and it was feeling so good now.

"I could come like this," she whispered, resting her forehead against his.

He angled up and kissed her again, dragging her against him until the heat between her legs was almost unbearable. Only then did he pull her up and slide the head of his cock inside of her. It was a smooth, easy motion, and as he pushed her down, down, down onto himself, he let off a guttural sound that was full of pleasure, and made her relax to take the rest of him.

When he was buried deep inside of her, he took a few moments to just hold her there, rolling his hips shallowly to keep the friction. Ooooh, he was good.

"I'm going to come already," she warned.

"Give it to me," he commanded, and she wanted to obey him.

She cupped his cheeks and tossed her head back, cried out as she came, gripping his dick so hard with the pulses of pleasure he caused.

"Goooood," he purred in a demon's voice. He pulled her against him over and over, dragging out every throbbing moment of her pleasure.

Panting, she rested her forehead against his shoulder and gripped his back. Gunner eased her back, and she arched her spine as he drew one of her sensitive nipples into his mouth. "Gunner," she whispered shakily.

"Mmmmmmm," he groaned, rolling his hips again.

He was so smooth, so strong. He knew just the right pace for her, and the tension inside of her body was already building again.

"Gunner," she said again, pleading.

"Fuck, I need it," he growled, gripping her hips hard. He slammed her against him—over and over, harder, faster—until she was screaming his name.

Her body exploded as he pulsed wet heat into her. He froze and grunted, eased her back, and then pulled her against him again, buried himself even deeper as he filled her.

Mindless, she moved with him, instinctively pulling every jet of warmth from his body.

Breathless, boneless, she fell into him and disappeared into the strength of his arms wrapped all the way around her.

Safe.

God, it had been so long since she'd felt safe.

She wanted to laugh, and rejoice, and cry.

He nudged her head off his shoulder with his jaw and pressed his lips to hers again as her body pulsed on. She slid her arms around him and hugged him tightly. She couldn't hurt him. He harbored inhuman strength, after all.

His hand slipped to her throat again and he eased her back, searched her eyes with that bi-colored, glowing gaze of his. He didn't say anything, but he didn't need to.

She smiled and ran her nails through his hair. "You aren't evil," she whispered.

Gunner pulled her against his chest and hugged her so tightly, she could barely breathe. She didn't even care. Who gave a shit about something as trivial as oxygen when he'd just made her feel whole for the first time in years.

And from the silence that emanated from him, from the lack of the growl, from the disappearance of the tension in his body, from the way he held her so tightly…she thought she had done something similar for him.

SEVEN

The wind whipped at the helmet she wore as Gunner sped down the mountain pass.

She was keeping her promise—she would require nothing of him.

She had been a cool girl as they had dressed. She had tossed him wicked smiles as she caught him staring at her over and over.

Hallie would make this easy on them.

No feelings, no attachments, no neediness.

At least, that's how she would appear to him.

She gripped his waist tighter as he hit a sharp turn, and tried not to imagine what would happen to them at this speed if a deer stepped into the road.

She'd always thought boys who rode motorcycles

didn't care if they lived or died, and meeting Gunner didn't ease that feeling.

He rode this because it made him feel alive in some strange way. The danger was the attractive part of it for him, and she kind of understood it.

She felt alive right now too.

He slowed behind a truck, and she tensed to prepare for him to speed around it, but he surprised her. He sat up straighter and coasted at seventy miles an hour behind the truck. She looked into the side-view mirror, and he was looking back at her with a thoughtful expression on his face. Oh, he was lost in his head too.

She wished he could see her soft smile.

He reached back, slid his hand against the side of her calf, and squeezed gently. She let off a huff of breath as she wrapped her arms more tightly around his waist.

She didn't know how she guessed, but she bet he wasn't an affectionate creature by nature.

He was doing her a kindness. Felt so good.

She rested the side of her helmet against his back. He pulled his hand away from her leg and pulled one of her hands up higher on his chest, held it there against his pounding heartbeat.

Oh, this man. This shifter. This mystery. This layered soul with so much heart, but he had good in him.

She didn't want to leave tomorrow.

She didn't want to leave, but she was also aware that her leaving was why tonight felt so potent. All they had was this short time together.

It was easy to tear down walls, demolish barriers, and be truthful with the grit of their lives. Why? Because they would likely never see each other again.

Their messes were safe.

He released her hand and patted her leg, telling her they were about to go fast. She held on tighter and ducked down behind him as he hit the next gear and blasted past the pickup truck. He drove her straight through town and to the police station. He came to a stop next to her car, and offered his hand to help her off.

"I'll follow you home, make sure you get there safe," he told her as she removed her helmet and gave it back.

"Oh, you don't have to do that."

"I would be fine without doing that if you weren't

being hunted," he said low as he pulled the helmet over his head.

She cupped the helmet and smiled, then flipped down his visor. "Tonight was my favorite."

She'd said it over her shoulder as she sauntered to her car, dragging the keys out of her purse as she went.

Hallie opened her door and stood in the opening. She sighed and canted her head. "I wish I would've met you three years ago."

She couldn't see his facial expression behind the mirrored visor, but he angled his helmet down, and she knew he understood what she was saying.

They'd met at the wrong time, after all the damage.

That part made her heart ache in ways she didn't understand.

He twitched his head. *Get in.*

She smiled one last time and blew him a kiss, then sank down into the car, started it, and aimed her car for Corey's property outside of town.

She stalled. She went five below the speed limit, her eyes constantly casting to the rearview mirror where the motorcycle followed behind her.

She really was terrible at goodbyes.

Already her eyes were burning and her heart was hurting.

When she came to the dirt-road turnoff to a cluster of rural properties, he paused at the for-sale sign in front of the Miller's old place. She slowed and stopped, watching him. He was sitting there frozen by the mailboxes, just...staring at that for-sale sign.

1010 Winding Creek Way had been for sale for years. It was a crap-hole. The cabin had been abandoned when she and Corey were children. No one had wanted to fuss with it way out here. Someone had bought it and let it sit for years, never did anything with it.

When he put the kickstand down, dismounted, and strode for her window, she was confused.

Hallie rolled the window down as he flipped his visor up and locked his arms against her car. "Stay one more day."

"What?"

"Stay one more day," he repeated.

"I..." Hallie frowned, mind racing. "It'll just make it harder to leave."

"You're tough," he told her, then pushed off the

car, pulled his helmet off, leaned inside, and kissed the devil out of her.

He eased back with a small smack of his lips and sauntered back to his motorcycle. "Stay one more day," he called without turning back around.

"And then what?" she called, hanging out the window.

"And then we'll see."

EIGHT

Hallie didn't know how to feel.

Corey waved as she loaded up into her car. "Have a good day at work!"

This was the part where Hallie was supposed to wave and tell her, "See you tonight," and then leave while Corey was at work, and later write her a long text apologizing for not staying when she was in some cheap motel in another state.

But here she was, dressed for work, hauling her giant coffee thermos, and definitely not leaving town.

This was all Gunner's fault.

She had been mentally prepared. She had been ready. She had accepted her fate!

And now she was heading to work like nothing

was amiss. Like her ex hadn't found her. Like he wouldn't ruin the life she'd built here and anyone who got close to her.

She was a damn grenade.

"This is such a bad idea," she muttered as she slid into her car.

The drive to work took half an hour, but today would be an easy day. Thank goodness, because she was exhausted from two nights of staying up thinking about a sexy shifter.

She'd tased him, and he'd still fucked her silly.

Hallie bit her lip against a grin. It had been an illuminating couple of days.

She couldn't be in a bad mood this morning if she tried. That man had consumed her last night, and her body was still buzzing from the high of him.

At the jobsite, she parked her car behind the others and grabbed her hard hat out of the front seat.

Before she left the car, she picked up her phone and confirmed her counseling appointment for later. Just as she moved to leave the car, a text came through.

Can we talk? It had been sent from an unknown number, but she already knew who it was from.

Derek had probably figured out he was blocked on her phone and was messaging from anther number.

Her stomach dropped to the floorboard of her car.

"Hallie, you coming?" Sam called from up ahead.

"Be right there," she called out the open door, but then dragged her gaze back to her phone.

I just want you to leave me alone. I'm happy. I want nothing to do with you. I'm dating someone. Move on, asshole. Send.

With trembling fingers, she held her phone and watched as the little dots said Derek was typing. Her heart was pounding so hard!

A video message came through. When she clicked play, it wasn't Derek sitting there looking confused. Gunner was rubbing his hand down the scruff on his face. "Geez, lady, you move on quick. It's not polite to call someone an asshole when they made you come twice last night. I'm going to go out on a limb and say that message wasn't for me. Just telling you good morning, and I wanted to tell you something." The humor faded from his eyes. "I'm taking your advice. I'm going to apologize. I was going to see if you wanted to come with me. After counseling, of course.

I remembered you saying it's Tuesdays and Thursdays, and today is Thursday. Take your time, go to your bar, process, get your shot of whiskey, and then let me know if you feel like meeting the Warlanders. It'll be ugly and uncomfortable." He scratched his neck and rested his arm on an open window. Was he in a pickup truck? Okay, hot-boy. "Last night was fun. Not the talking part, I mean the fucking part." The cheeky smile returned to his masculine lips. "You said you're dating someone. Better not be. I don't like sharing."

The video clicked off, and she sat there with her mouth hanging open. It hadn't been Derek who sent her that message at all. This was Gunner's number. He'd gotten her number from the message to Bangaboarlander! Aaaaah! She stomped her feet in quick succession on the floorboard and squealed with happiness.

"Hallie!" Sam called.

"Fuck off, I still have five minutes!" she belted out, and tossed a middle finger up for good measure. The boys on her crew were ridiculously needy sometimes.

She aimed the camera function on her phone at her face. Before she hit record, she fluffed her hair and got a good angle. She hit record. "Hi, hello, hi." She grinned. "Good morning. Ummmm, I thought you were Derek. I'm not really dating anyone, I was just saying that." She grinned like a weirdo. "Okay, all that to say, I would love to go to your apology party with you. What should I bring? Wine? Beer? What do the Warlanders like? What can I do to soften the apology? We can be a team. Teamwork!"

"Hallie!" Sam yelled.

"I'm busy!" she yelled back, then smiled brightly at the camera. "Um, I have to get to work." She reached over, grabbed her hard hat, and put it on her head. "Very important stuff to accomplish today." She tapped her hard hat and cheesed at the camera. "Don't miss me too badly. I'll tell my therapist all about you. She'll probably tell me to run, and I'll ignore her sage advice. I can say with confidence that so far, you are my favorite mistake. See you soon."

She gave a megawatt grin and stopped recording, then sent the video to Gunner before she got out and threw an empty soda can at Sam's stupid head because he was standing in front of her car pelvic thrusting.

Boys could be so stupid.

NINE

Gunner watched her video for the third time in a row. God, she was so damn cute. He liked that she could be spicy and tell a coworker to piss off, then bring that bright smile right back for him.

That woman was trouble in so many more ways than she understood.

He lifted his gaze to the dilapidated cabin in front of his truck. There wasn't even a yard. It was just overgrown brush that said nature had taken this property back years ago.

1010 Winding Creek Way. Did that suggest there was a creek? He pushed open his door and stepped out of his truck. He'd figured the motorcycle might have some trouble getting up here. He'd called the realtor this morning, and she'd basically told him to just make any offer and it would be considered. This place had been abandoned for years. Half the damn roof on the small cabin was caved in, and he started mentally calculating how much the repairs and cleanup on this place would be.

The cabin might honestly be a complete teardown, and then he would have to start from scratch. He had savings, but it wouldn't cover a new home build.

A vision flashed against his mind and shot blinding pain through his skull.

...walking through the woods...

...looking behind him...

...his pawprints in the mud...

Jerkily, Gunner stumbled toward the tree line. This was the part he hated. He'd been enjoying a peaceful moment where he could fantasize over life feeling normal someday, and the bear had taken his body.

He slapped his head hard a few times, but his legs kept pushing forward and a long snarl filled his chest.

Fuck, he wished he was normal. Wished he was human.

The woods were thick and overgrown. He stumbled and tripped past brambles and briars until he could hear water.

True to the street name, a creek rushed down the slight slope of the terrain.

Only now, at the bank, did the bear stop and rip him down to his knees in the mud.

Look.

Gunner pitched forward onto his hands and knees, his fingertips in the water. His reflection looked back at him, but he wasn't a man. He was the bear. When he looked down at his hands, they weren't hands at all anymore. They were enormous paws with six-inch black claws as sharp as daggers.

He'd Changed?

Shit. He hadn't even realized.

He huffed a breath and backed away from the water, tried to adjust to walking on all fours.

Angry at having his body stolen, he forced a Change back. It was slow and painful, but it was what he deserved.

When he came to, his head was pounding.

Gunner rolled to his back and stared up at the full tree branches above. A raven flew across the sky, and then another, both cawing loudly.

His body ached. He frowned as he took in the sky. The sun was in a completely different position than when he'd come out here.

He sat up with a gasp. How long had he been here?

He only remembered a few minutes, but the aching in his body said he'd been a bear for a while.

"Fuck," he murmured as he pushed himself upward. He stormed back through brush that had been cleared. It smelled like his bear here, and the woods were familiar, as if he'd already memorized it.

"Dammit! Why can't you just let me feel normal?" he yelled, his voice echoing through the forest.

By the time he got back to his truck and turned it on, the clock said he'd been here for four hours. He huffed a humorless laugh, hating himself. This happened way too much.

Lucas should've just put him down when he had the chance.

Gunner rested his head back against the seat and closed his eyes. Everything had gotten so messed up with the Warlanders, and he knew it was on him. Everything was on him and his fucked-up animal.

They had almost...*almost*...felt like friends there for a little while.

Tonight was going to be impossible. His only chance of getting through what he needed to do was to have Hallie there. Why? Because his bear got quiet around her. Maybe he could keep his mind long enough to own the destruction he'd caused.

I like it here. He didn't know how he could understand the animal. It was all in his mind, and there was no way bears could really speak the same language as him, but he understood all the same. Always had.

"You don't matter," Gunner gritted out as he started the truck.

I like it here, the animal repeated.

Gunner wouldn't say it out loud, and was trying very hard not to think it, but he did too. Dilapidated cabin and all.

It was overgrown and wild, unloved and uncared for. He glanced in the rearview mirror one last time as he pulled away.

The 1010 had to mean something, didn't it?

A text came through, vibrating his phone in the cupholder. When he lifted it up to check if it was

Hallie, he was surprised by the name on the ID.

Lucia had texted, *Getting warmer.*

Gunner pursed his lips against a smile and set the phone back into the cupholder. He secretly liked having a little cheerleader. For some reason, Lucia's faith in him gave him moments where he had a little faith in himself too. Hallie also served as a motivation, but he couldn't explain that part yet. He'd just met her. She was a stranger.

No she isn't.

Gunner shook his head. This shit right here was why he didn't drive his truck much anymore. It was too relaxing, and his mind drifted into the bear's possession too much. On the motorcycle he had to be hyperaware, and the bear grew quieter the faster he went.

He aimed for town and drove straight through, headed for the cheap motel he'd paid a few nights on. He needed food, and there was a little diner attached to it that served a decent steak. He needed red meat. The Changes made him feel like he was starving, and apparently he'd been Changed for freaking hours today. Not on purpose.

There was traffic ahead, and he guided his truck

toward the inside lane to try and see around the line of cars. Up ahead there were a bunch of work trucks pulled to the side. Construction. Crap. He checked his blind spot to pull a U-turn and take a different way, but just then the car in front of him started pulling forward, so he stayed in line.

He pulled up slowly, and when he saw the flagger, he hit the brake.

Hallie was holding a *Slow* sign and gesturing cars past.

She worked construction? As a flagger?

It was her. She had her long, dark hair in a low ponytail under her hard hat. She wore thick work pants that cinched at her waist and thick-soled work boots. Makeup all done up, she was looking sexier than he'd ever seen a woman look before.

She frowned at his truck and gestured him forward. He eased onto the gas, rolled down the passenger's side window, and gave a catcall whistle.

"Hey, asshole—" The words died in her throat as she peered through the open window and saw him.

"That's the second time you've called me an asshole today."

She spun the sign around, and it read *Stop* now.

She lifted a walkie to her lips and said, "Hey, that's all for now. Take a turn."

"I only have three cars stacked," a grumpy voice sounded from the other end.

"Congratulations to those three cars then," Hallie barked.

God, she was gorgeous.

"You," she said to Gunner. "I know you."

He leaned onto the console and ran his hand down his facial scruff. "And I know every inch of you."

A red hue tinged her cheeks in an instant, and her pretty hazel eyes went wide. "You sure do. Oh my gosh," she whispered, pressing the back of the hand holding the walkie talkie to her pink cheeks as she checked the cars coming this way.

"You work construction?" he asked. "Do you even understand how hot that is to a guy like me?"

"I don't hate that you're a logger, either. I like them blue-collar boys."

"I'll have to find another logging job then," he said. Gah, she was easy to flirt with.

Her cheeks were turning a darker shade of pink, and he freaking loved this.

"What are you up to?" she asked.

"Uuuum…" He frowned at the last of the three cars passing in the other lane. Honesty was best with this one. She didn't judge, and he liked testing her. "I just Changed into my bear in a territory that does not belong to me. On accident."

"Your bear sounds like a troublemaker."

"Mmm. His nickname is Fury."

"Okay, that's a hot-boy nickname."

He chuckled and shook his head. "Your instincts are broken."

She pulled her phone up, and a click sounded.

"Did you just take a picture?" he asked.

"Yep. You look good." Hallie grinned brightly and smoothly turned the sign to *Slow*. "Make like a cow and mooooove."

"Terrible joke."

"And yet you're smiling. See you real soon, Furry."

"It's Fury." He eased forward, but then stopped again on a whim. "Come here," he called.

Hallie jogged to catch up to him, threw open his passenger's side door, and locked her arm on the seat. "What do you want?" she asked, pursing her lips against a smile.

"I want to fuck you, but you're working, so I'll

settle for something quick."

A satisfied smile spread across her pretty face, and then she leaned forward and pressed her lips to his with a quick *smack* sound that had his dick throbbing against his jeans.

She eased back to the chattering on the walkie talkie and waved him off.

He checked the mirror as he coasted through the lane created by orange cones. She was standing in her position with the sign back in place, her eyes on his truck. She wore the prettiest smile he'd ever seen.

Whoooo, that woman was dangerous.

Sure, she might only be here until tomorrow, but he had another entire night of distraction, and he was going to soak up every second of it.

TEN

Hallie wiped the tears from her cheeks and inhaled roughly. It was hard to draw a breath with everything happening in her head.

She rested her forehead against the steering wheel and fell apart, shoulders shaking. It hadn't hit her until she'd gotten to the parking lot of that little hole-in-the-wall bar what she'd actually admitted to in her counseling session.

What was she doing? What the hell was she still doing here?

She wiped her eyes with the sleeves of her hoodie and gritted out, "Get it together." She huffed three steadying breaths and then pushed her door open. She pulled the hood of her hoodie over her hair and slipped the sleeves over her hands, crossed her arms, and strode for the front door.

This bar was always dead at this time of day, and thank God for small blessings. She forced a smile for the bartender, but he twitched his chin toward her table in the corner by the window.

A man sat at it with his back to her.

Gunner was staring out the window toward where her car was parked.

She was stunned into stillness. "Gunner?"

He didn't turn around, only pushed the seat across from him out for her with his foot.

There were two shots of whiskey already on the table.

She didn't know how to feel. He was intruding on a private, awful moment, but…but…a part of her was relieved he was here.

Slowly, she made her way to the chair and sank down into it, stared out the window with him. Oh, he probably had the perfect view of her falling apart in her car.

"Did you see me?" she asked softly.

"Yes." There was a growl in his voice.

She dragged her gaze to him and wiped her

cheeks again. "I'm sorry."

"Do you want me to kill him?" he asked, dragging his gaze to her. His pupils were constricted, so his bright silver-and-blue eyes looked even brighter. His skin was slightly red, as if he was angry, and the angles of his face looked sharper. "Now?"

She knew his offer was genuine. It should terrify her, but for some reason it didn't. She appreciated that there was someone in the world who would avenge her if anything ever happened.

Hallie leaned forward, her elbows on the table and her hands pressed to her cheeks. She wanted to hide her tearstained face from him, but he pulled one of her hands down and just held it.

"What can I do?" he asked. "I have to do something."

She shook her head. "Sometimes I just need you to sit with me."

He searched her eyes, and at last, nodded once. He leaned back in his chair and released her hand, lifted the shot and downed it, then looked to the bartender and nodded for another.

She didn't know how long they sat like that—quiet, just existing together. Her thoughts were spinning around and around, and she was so confused by herself.

He was watching her, tearing up a napkin. His face was an unreadable mask, some combination of anger and softness.

Her counselor had said it was the first time she'd seen a real smile from her, and it had started a flood of emotions like an avalanche.

Hallie took her shot, wincing as the amber liquor burned all the way down. "I've been numb for a long time."

Gunner didn't say anything. He just kept slowly ripping the napkin into tiny pieces of confetti. It was exactly what she needed.

She cleared her throat and wiped away two more tears that spilled over. "I don't know why I'm crying. I'm fine." She laughed thickly. "I told my counselor about you."

He looked as if he wanted to say something, but swallowed hard and frowned down at the napkin.

"I was telling her about you, and she told me it was the first time my eyes have had some life in them. It was the first time she had seen me smile. I showed her the video I had sent you today, and she watched it twice. She said she didn't even recognize that girl in the video, and it hit me how heavy I've felt for so long. The realization that I was myself again, if only for a few minutes, it just felt so big. And it also made the stuff that dragged me down feel so big. I'm okay. I'm okay." Her face crumpled and she squeezed her hands together under the table, digging her nails into her palms to punish herself. *Get it together!* "I guess yesterday, and today, were the happiest days I've had in a long time. It's been nice. It's also been terrifying," she admitted. "It'll end, and I'll have to go back to making myself numb and not connecting with people, and running, and always feeling like a burden, and feeling like I'm...nothing. This would've been easier if you just didn't show up last night. Now I'll have to put myself back in the cage, and it'll hurt." She wiped her stupid tears again. Her eyes were just constantly leaking. "I don't really like feeling like I'm in a cage."

"Make me understand why," he said low, but his voice was all growl.

It should scare her, right? He sounded like a demon.

"Why I'm in a cage?"

He nodded, eyes on the destroyed napkin in his hands.

He hadn't taken his second shot, so she reached across the table and pulled it to herself, tipped it back and took it, winced again. She nodded to the bartender for another round for both of them.

"I have an admission."

"Say it."

"Yesterday I was comfortable with telling you every dark part of my life. I didn't care. I would never see you again, but now it feels different. I want to hide so that when I leave, you can think fondly of me."

He cracked his knuckles and leaned forward on his elbows, scanned the bar, and then leveled her with those glowing two-colored eyes. "I'm not interested in thinking fondly of some fake version of you. I'd rather know the real. I'm not interested in perfect, Hallie. I'm not perfect. Why would I seek someone who is?"

"I want you to like me," she admitted in a whisper as she wiped another stupid tear away with the sleeve of her hoodie.

He didn't say more, and leaned back as the bartender set two shots of whiskey between them.

She inhaled deeply, and told him, "I'm different than I used to be. I was social, never met a stranger. Grew up poor, but it didn't matter. I had a solid friend group. I learned to work early, and I learned to be charming. I was serving tables in restaurants by the time I was fifteen. Quit school so I could work and help my mom pay bills. I worked my way up to more and more expensive restaurants, and do you know what I was interested in when I dated men?"

"Money?" he guessed.

"Money," she admitted, disgusted. "I didn't want to work doubles all my life. I didn't want to live in roach-infested houses forever. When I got a job at the best steakhouse in Kansas City, I thought my ship had come in. The bills were huge, so the tips were also big. I could make more in one shift than I could in a week at my other jobs. I kept my head down and worked. One day, a big group of businessmen came into the restaurant and sat in my section, and I saw dollar signs. They were ordering everything, the best of the best, all the drinks. Drinks upon drinks all night. They sat in my section for hours, but I didn't mind because their bill was getting bigger and bigger. One of the men there was clearly with a date, but he kept staring at me. My manager asked if I knew who he was, and when I told her I didn't, she got this smile on her face. She said treat him well, and he would treat me well. So I did. I made sure to cater to everything his party needed. The woman he was with seemed irritated with his attention on me, but I wasn't seeking that attention. When she started being rude to me, I understood. I wouldn't want my man paying attention to another woman either." She uncrossed and recrossed her legs under the table. "It turns out Derek owned the restaurant. Eventually I figured out that meant he thought he owned me. I said yes to too much. It started small. He would come in near the end of my shift and work on his laptop at the bar. He would ask me to talk for a few minutes as my boss was closing up and the chefs were prepping the kitchen for the next day. At first it was easygoing, but he was flirty. I asked him about the woman he'd come in with, and he said he'd broken up with her. I asked him why, and he said he found someone he liked better. And I'll admit, it was very exciting. I was nobody, you know? I was just working to make ends meet, and finally making enough that I had money leftover each week. I could pay my bills and have money to buy clothes. When you serve tables, you live mostly on tips. The paychecks are taxed, so it would be just a little bit leftover after taxes, but after a couple of months, my paycheck was thousands of dollars. I couldn't believe it. I took my mom and all my friends out that night. And the paychecks kept coming in. Any time Derek sat in my section he would leave a thousand-dollar tip, and it was a transition that I was fine with. I was thirsty for it. Felt like everything was falling into place. He seemed nice, so the first time he put a move on me, I was ready. I was happy. He was a powerful man, and had his hand in so much in the town I'd grown up in. He was only a few years older than me, and handsome, and he made me believe he was taking care of me and always would and I...I...got caught up in it, you know?"

She dared a glance up at Gunner's face, but he was just watching her with his head cocked to the side like some curious animal. She couldn't read his expression. Was he disappointed in her? Was he disgusted?

"Anyway, that went on for months, but he changed over time. It was easy at first, but then he started wanting to know everywhere I was.

Everything I was doing. He had me download this app on my phone that would give him my exact location, but he didn't share his location with me. He would show up at the restaurant all times of the day and just cause tension. He would cause fights over nothing. I had to act and be perfect, but his version of perfect was reading his mind and obeying his thousand rules that he made up as he went. It seemed like the more he cared for me, the more possessive he got. He didn't just want to take care of me. He wanted to own me. He kept tabs on everything he did for me, and used them any time I was trying to tell him I wasn't happy. I tried to leave, and the next day my boss brought me into the office and said my position at the restaurant was in jeopardy. Not only that, but Derek would make sure I never worked in any of the nice restaurants in that town again. He and his family knew everyone. He started buying me clothes and toting me around, but even when we went out, he didn't let me out of his sight. And if any man talked to me, even his friends, he would fly into a rage. I found out the woman he'd been with that first night had been his fiancée. He'd thrown her away to pursue me, and it had caused a huge rift in his family and business relations. He held that over my head. Said I owed him loyalty because he'd given up so much for me. And little by little, I was buying it. I was getting trapped, and I didn't know how to get out. The first time he hit me, I swore to myself I would leave. And then four-dozen roses showed up at the penthouse apartment he'd set me up in, and the manipulation began. I had never been through anything like that. It would get really bad, and then he would be so good to me and bring me back in line. And then it would start to get bad again. I couldn't do anything right, he would cause fights, he would go out drinking with his friends, he would show up at my place begging me to ease his demons, and then I would get hurt, and on and on and on it went."

"Where was your mom in all of this?" he asked softly. "Where were your friends?"

"They were telling me I was being dramatic when I would try to leave. They would tell me I needed to try harder. His wealth was trickling down to them. He knew what he was doing. He treated them well out the gate, and then they were on his side. They would listen to whatever charming thing he said, ignore the bruises on my face, and tell me it was a small price to pay."

"Those weren't friends."

"Those weren't friends," she agreed.

"Does your mom regret encouraging it?"

She shrugged as another wave of pain took her. "I don't know. I haven't talked to her since I left Kansas City. If I was going to leave, I had to go cold-turkey. He would get information from the people I used to know. Their loyalty shifted to him over time. I knew it. I could feel it. I just got quiet as I listened to them defend his actions." She inhaled deeply. "The night he broke my nose, you know what he told me?"

Gunner's hands were fisted on the table, and a steady growl emanated from him. He didn't say anything.

"He squeezed my jaw and made me look at myself in the mirror, and he said that I deserved it." Two more tears fell to her cheeks. Frustrated, she dashed the damp sleeve of her hoodie over her face. "I don't know why I'm crying. I dealt with this a long time ago. I don't cry over this shit anymore."

"You were bleeding?"

"Gushing. I said I really needed to go the hospital, and he told me he wanted me to remember my disobedience and the consequences every time I looked in the mirror. He said my ruined face would make sure that no one else would want me. That I was bound to him now."

"How long from then until you left him?" Gunner asked.

"Too long. I was so scared and just...stuck. I felt trapped and I still don't know why I couldn't escape it. He was so deep in my head. One night it happened again, and I went to my mom for help, told her what he'd done, and do you know what she did?"

Gunner shook his head.

"She defended him. His money meant a lot to her. He was supporting her too by that time. My heart went cold to her that day. I felt so betrayed and alone, and by that night, I was packed up, had cashed out my bank account, and was searching for cheap motels. I'd been putting money away, saving, preparing to disappear. I hoped he would forget about me when he lost sight of me, but he is a hunter."

"Stalker," Gunner murmured.

"He's found all of my hiding places, but I lasted longest here in Laramie with Corey. Four months of freedom here. I even started to feel safe again, but he has a big reach."

"*Had* a big reach."

She inhaled deeply and stared out the window at her car. "He's connected. His family runs that city. He's not a man who accepts losing, and to him, a little no-name waitress rejected him."

"Why do you work construction now?"

She forced a smile. "They'll pay in cash if I don't have all my paperwork in order. He can't track cash. If I go to a restaurant, they need my information for taxes. He always finds me."

"Your life isn't over, you know," Gunner told her.

She couldn't explain why, but those words meant a lot to her. "Do you think less of me?"

Gunner puffed air out of his cheeks and took his last shot. He leaned back in his chair and linked his hands behind his head. "I think even less of Derek, which is a feat. I already wanted to torture him. Now it's all I'll think about." He stared at her for a four-count and then said, "No, I don't think less of you. You fell for someone with more money and power than you. You're not the first person in the world to fall into that. I paired up with my friend's mate."

Hallie's face went slack. "I need to know all of the

details."

He snorted, cracked his neck this way and that, and then leaned forward again. "When I was young, in high school, I was in Damon's Mountains, and all the kids had grown up together. Lucas was my friend. He was a gorilla shifter, a blackback at the time, but he would be a monster someday. My grizzly was dominant and coming into his own, and as we got older, the relationship turned competitive. He dated this tiger shifter named Cadence for years, but his animal didn't bond to her. Anyone could see it. Her animal was addicted to him, but he stayed distant. It didn't work. Over time, I started seeing the good parts of her, and I was there when she would cry about Lucas. I got protective. Worse, my animal got protective, and I started to hate Lucas. It was a slow, poisonous thing. Cadence came to me the week after Lucas broke it off for good, and I gave in. I'd wanted her for so long, and she was there, asking for comfort, throwing herself at me, and I just..." He shook his head. "I knew I could do it better than Lucas." Gunner shrugged. "She regretted being with me quick, and stupid me, I'd thought it was real. My grizzly bonded to her. Cadence was a wreck from bonding to Lucas, and then I did the same damn thing. That's called karma. I had an eye for my friend's mate. The aftermath destroyed my animal."

"When you choose a mate, it's only one?"

"Ask me that a couple years ago, I would've answered yes, but I watched Cadence move on with someone new. She bonded to Kru easy."

"Watched it?" she asked softly.

He chewed the corner of his lip and nodded. "Lucas, Cadence, and Kru are all in the Warlanders."

"Holy shit," she whispered, her mind racing. "Your Crew has a love triangle in it?"

"It's not a love triangle. None of us ended up paired together. Lucas ended up with Jenna, Cadence ended up with Kru. Even Lucia found a mate."

"Oh my God, I am now very invested in this soap opera. Who is Lucia?"

He scrunched up his face. "She's a grizzly shifter. And she can see the future. So anyway, I lost my damn mind and all my control over my animal. I ended up trying to kill them all, and the scuffle set the entire trailer park on fire, and now I'm the outcast of Damon's Mountains. You fucked a winner."

She belted a laugh that was so loud, it surprised

even her.

"You have as bad a taste in relationships as me."

"It's a gift," he said sarcastically.

Well, she wasn't crying anymore. Now she was utterly distracted from her own mental constipation by thinking of the shit-show that was his former Crew.

"Okay, so I'm going to meet your ex...mate? Today?"

"If she's home. I can't exactly call them and give them a heads-up. Most of them blocked me."

Hallie pursed her lips against a laugh.

"It's not funny," he assured her.

"Right," she agreed, biting back a grin.

Gunner crossed his arms over his chest. "It's not something we should be laughing at."

"You're a shit-show."

"Oh, an insult from another shit-show?"

She giggled and took a sip of a water the bartender had brought. "Whose story is worse?"

"I would not like to do a competition," he said easily, and now she could see a smile tugging at the corners of his lips.

At least he had a sense of humor that could

lighten a heavy moment. There was value in that to a woman like her.

"Next time we fuck, wear the hard hat," he uttered, and she nearly choked on the water.

"Gunner," she warned as a trio of men walked by to take their seats at the table beside them. The bar was beginning to get busier.

"Maybe your work boots, too." He gave her a hungry look. "No pants, just bent over a bed getting railed from behind by a blue-collar boy. No tips."

"Check please," she called.

He tossed his head back and laughed, and God, what that sound did to settle her. He had a great laugh.

"Feel better?" he asked, the smile still lingering on his lips.

"Much better. Thank you for listening."

"That was terrible."

"You're used to action?"

"Yes. You were crying."

"Sometimes women just need someone to listen."

"Torture. I'm a man of action."

The buzz from the whiskey felt good, and she scanned the parking lot. "Where's that truck you were driving?"

"I parked it at my motel. That thing is brutal. It's too quiet."

"You know, my mom once told me that men who ride motorcycles are just tempting death."

"I fuckin' know. So far Death is ignoring me."

"Like your romantic relationships, heyoooo," she crowed.

"I know someone who can fix your nose," he said suddenly, the smile drifting from his face.

She stilled. "Who?"

"Lucia's mate is a healer. I would bet my boots he could reset it."

She rested her chin on her palm and smiled. "I'll think about it. Lately I kind of like the reminder."

"What reminder?" he asked carefully.

"The reminder that I'm a motherfucking survivor."

A slow smile stretched his lips, and he nodded. "Attagirl."

"Does it bother you?" she asked seriously.

Gunner stared at her for a few moments and then stood, offered his hand, and pulled her up. He slipped his hand over her throat and gently pulled her in, hesitated an inch from her, then kissed her nose. "No. It reminds me that you're a motherfucking survivor."

He released her and she rocked forward, breathless. Stunned, she watched him pull his wallet out and throw down cash for their drinks and a big tip for the bartender. He reached for her hand easily and led her out of the bar.

She looked down at where her small hand was held in his big, strong one, and for a moment, the butterflies in her stomach were overwhelming. She'd never felt like this with anyone in her life.

He could take her worst admissions and shrug them off, then make her feel better about them.

And then he could make her insecurities disappear completely with a simple kiss.

Oooooh, a woman like her could get real loyal to a dangerous man like him.

He led her out of the bar and told her to lock her car, which she did. Then he strode toward his motorcycle, and time slowed as she watched him make his way to the black-on-black bike with two helmets sitting on the seat. He was wearing a forest green T-shirt today with dark-wash jeans and a chain wallet. It was like a slow-motion movie scene as he pulled his helmet over his face and angled it toward her as he buckled it under his chin. She could see her stunned look in the reflection of his mirrored visor.

This man was so fine.

He picked up the other helmet and held it out, and she realized what he had done.

The full-face helmet was shiny and brand-new, with red detailing and a mirrored silver visor.

"Where did you get this?" she asked, taking it from his hand.

"Try it on so I can make sure I got the right size."

She pulled it over her head and it was tight, but settled comfortably over her face. The visor was up, so she got a perfect view of him buckling it under her chin. Then he flipped her visor down, gripped her helmet under the chin, and angled her head up. He pressed his helmet to hers like a kiss, and her knees locked.

Gunner slid his leg over the seat of his motorcycle and then offered his hand. She was much more graceful at climbing the peg and mounting behind him this time. When her arms were settled around his waist, he pulled out.

"Can you hear me?" he asked.

Startled with his voice right in her ear, Hallie tensed and gripped his shirt. "Yes! Can you hear me?"

"Yep."

"Oh my gosh! Is it speakers?"

He chuckled and pulled to a stop at a newly-red light. "What kind of music do you like?" he asked, messing with his phone that was mounted between the handlebars.

"I want to feel like a badass!"

He laughed and nodded. "You are a badass."

"Cowboys from Hell" by Pantera started playing, and she clenched her fists in the air. "I love this song!"

"Of course you do." There was a smile in his voice, and he locked his arms on the handlebars again and looked to the side. There was a minivan beside them, and a little boy was waving to them out the window.

The woman driving said, "My son loves motorcycles," out of her open window.

Gunner revved the engine loudly, and the kiddo went crazy in the van.

"Oh my gosh, thank you," the mom said.

Gunner guided the motorcycle over to the van and pressed his fist against the window. The little boy stopped cheering to put his little fist on the window, and oh Mylanta...Hallie was melting.

She'd seen Gunner take a bullet and laugh. She'd seen Gunner nearly kill someone following her. She'd seen Gunner near a panic attack, and she'd seen Gunner go hungry when he fucked her.

Now she'd seen his reaction to a kid, and she blew out a breath. That man, that man!

His every layer was sexy.

He revved it a couple more times as the light turned green, and Hallie melted over the kid's cheering. Then she held on because Gunner patted her leg. Last night that had meant he was going to gun it, and he did. She was right. Only this time wasn't quite as terrifying because she trusted him more and knew what to expect.

He slowed and eased into the parking lot of a motel, parked in front of room 101, and helped her off.

"Nice house," she said cheekily as she pulled her helmet off and followed him into the room.

"Thanks. It does the job while I figure out where I want to go."

"Sounds like we're both on the run."

He hissed an inhale. "I burned my old home to the

ground a few weeks ago."

"Whoa, that wasn't long ago."

"Nope."

The door swung closed as Gunner removed his helmet and set it on the dresser. The room was clean and tidy, and the bed was made. The artwork on the wall was generic and boring, and the lighting was dim. "Looks like we both gave the middle finger to our old lives."

"You're used to something nicer," he said softly.

"No! No, no, no, party foul," she told him, flopping onto the bed with her arms and legs spread like a starfish. "You can't use my old life against me, and I'm not allowed to use your old life against you. Them's the rules."

"I like that rule," he murmured, leaning against the dresser and canting his head as he looked at her. "It's not usually like this for me though."

She rolled onto her side and propped her cheek on her palm. "You aren't pressuring me. And you aren't keeping tabs on me. You have a roof over your head. I'm staying in a spare bedroom at my cousin's house. Like I said, I've been humbled a thousand times. This…" She looked around. "This feels like freedom to me."

"You like money," he said.

"I used to. Now, money gets me caught. It catches the attention of my hunter. I'm happy when I feel safe."

"And do you feel safe?" he asked softly.

"Yes."

His eyebrow arched up. "With me?"

"I saw the smile on your face after you were shot, Gunner. It's burned into my mind. I'm happy to be on your good side."

A slow, calculating smile commandeered his face, showing just the hint of a dimple on his right cheek. He lifted his chin higher and pushed off the dresser, sauntered over to her, and fell on top of her. He kept his weight off her with his locked arms, and raked his hungry gaze up and down her body. "No one on this earth will ever hurt you when I'm around." He leaned down and brushed his lips over her sensitive earlobe. "If you were a shifter, you would hear the truth in my oath as I said that. You." He kissed her earlobe. "Are." He kissed her throat. "Safe."

Gunner pressed his lips to hers and she melted back against the mattress, spread her knees instinctively so that he could settle his hips between her thighs. He grabbed her upper thigh and rolled his hips against hers as he pushed his tongue past her lips. Good…gaaaah…this man knew how to move over a woman.

She could let her mind go under his care. There was no thinking. She just did as he asked, knowing he would take care of her body.

He pulled her shirt and hoodie over her head and pulled her bra down, popping her breasts out of the top of the cups. He pulled one into his mouth and massaged the other. Mmmm, he liked her tits.

She cupped the sides of his head and rolled her head back, arched her back to meet the movement of his lips.

Gunner pushed upward and pulled his shirt over his head, let it drop to the corner of the bed, and fell back on her, skin against skin. He settled his weight onto her, but she'd already gotten an eyeful. His six-pack had rippled with his breath, his shoulders were tensed, his biceps were perfect. The line between his defined pecs belonged to some model in a magazine.

Yet here he was in all of his glory—his mess, his perfections and imperfections—focused on her body, and she felt lucky. She felt sexy.

Crooked nose and all, she felt beautiful.

He pushed her hands above her head as he rolled his body against hers, and intertwined his fingers with hers. His kiss had her closing her eyes and wishing for this to never end.

He took his time, primed her body, got her wet as he moved over her, against her, with her.

When he reached for her phone, she was only confused for a moment. "Pull the video up," he rumbled against her throat.

She'd never done this. She'd never done this! Excitement took her middle. "I trust you," she whispered, because it settled her to speak aloud.

"You can," he murmured, and gently nipped his teeth against her throat.

She opened the video. He pushed off her, set the phone on the chair by the window facing them, and then hit record. He returned to her, his back to the camera, and slowly, he pulled the zipper down on his jeans, eyes burning into her.

For a few moments, she thought about the video. She would watch this later. Did she look good? She messed with her hair, but he smiled and shook his head. "Don't change a damn thing. You're perfect."

Those words settled something inside of her chest. She relaxed back and watched him undress. When he knelt over her with nothing on, she drank in his Adonis body, and gave him a wicked grin as he reached forward and tugged at her leggings. He was smooth about it. Just peeled them right off over her ankles and then dropped them onto the floor. She was with him, here in this moment, vulnerable, no clothes on.

He eased himself over her and angled his face as he settled his lips near her ear again. "Don't think."

Hallie released a long, shuddering breath and closed her eyes as he dragged his hand down her ribs to her waist, and squeezed. He flipped her fast, with a strength that drew a gasp from her lips. She was on her stomach, looking at the pillows of the bed, and he was behind her, grasp on her hips as he lowered down to her.

His chest was warm against her back. He gripped her hair gently, angled her head back, and dragged kisses down her jawline to her neck. "So beautiful when you're open like this," he rumbled.

Gunner dragged her to the edge of the bed and

settled her feet onto the carpet, and then asked her, "Ready?"

On instinct, Hallie arched her back for him, angling her ass upward so he could slide into her easier.

"Gooood girl," he murmured near her ear, and she loved this. Loved every second of it.

Camera completely forgotten, she got lost in the moment as he slid his swollen cock into her from behind. His rumbled words of encouragement about what a good girl she was for taking all of him made her feel like a goddess.

He slid into her deep and eased back slower—in deep and fast, back slow. The best part...the very best part...was him saying, "I've got you," as he reached around her hips and pressed his fingertips to the most sensitive part of her. With a moan, she sagged forward, and he allowed it. He grabbed her hair and arched her back, but it wasn't painful. He was gentle. He knew how to cause pleasure, not pain. She could feel his powerful frame behind her, and she got completely lost in his care. Harder, faster. "Come on," he growled. "Come for me." She liked obeying him in these moments. Her body wanted to please him, and in doing so, she found a more intense pleasure.

She cried out as her body constricted and gripped his cock with her release.

He was ramming into her so hard now, her breasts were bouncing against the mattress.

She lost her mind. She had no idea what she was yelling, only that it felt better if she was loud.

The sexy sounds of pleasure that came from Gunner spurred her on, and her body pulsed on and on as he drove deep into her. And when he was close, she could tell, because his powerful body bucked into her and held as heat rushed into her.

He emptied himself completely inside of her, whispering against her ear how well she'd done. She was boneless.

He eased out of her and headed straight for the phone, eyes on the camera.

As he turned it off, Hallie lay with her face against the mattress, a soft smile of satisfaction on her lips.

He tossed the phone on the bed near her face.

"If your ex ever messages you again, you can respond with that."

Chills rippled up her spine at the snarl in his chest.

Oooooh, Gunner was possessive too, only this one didn't scare her.

The smile returned to her lips. She liked that he was willing to claim her like that.

Inhaling deeply, she rolled her eyes closed and enjoyed the last of the fading orgasm. Gunner returned with a washrag he had drenched with warm water, and he cleaned her gently. Hallie had never been a part of anything so intimate. This was more than sex now. He was taking care of her after. He hadn't just left her to feel empty or confused afterward. He had his big strong hand resting on her back as he washed her inner thighs.

Good man.

When Hallie rolled over, he lay beside her and pulled her in close, just held her against his stone-hard chest, where she could hear the cadence of his pounding heartbeat.

"You like me," she whispered.

"You shouldn't want that," he responded softly.

Perhaps not, but she did. The heart wanted what it wanted, and hers liked a big, beastly, dangerous man who made her feel taken care of.

This would make saying goodbye harder, but the

damage was done. Or was it repair? She didn't feel that all-too-familiar scared feeling here, in the dim light of his room.

All she felt with Gunner was freedom.

ELEVEN

"This was a bad idea."

The steering wheel creaked under Gunner's iron grip.

He had come to a stop at the top of a hill, on a one-lane gravel road, under a sign that read *Smashland Mobile Park.*

Ahead of them, a firepit was lit in the middle of a circle drive, and there were people gathered around it in different colored plastic chairs, staring at Gunner's truck, unmoving.

One of them was standing off to the side. He was an enormous man, like Gunner, and had his arms crossed over his chest, staring at the truck with eyes that glowed a strange gold color.

"Apologies aren't meant to be easy," she murmured.

"I shouldn't have brought you here," he rumbled. Already the human had faded from his voice.

He shifted gears to reverse, and she had to make a fast decision.

"Don't leave me here," she said quickly as she shoved the door open. She nearly fell as she hit the moving ground, and beside her, the truck jerked to a stop.

"Hallie, what the hell?" Gunner asked, his eyes blazing lighter.

Steeling herself, she forced her shaking legs to move. She jogged because she could hear Gunner's truck thrown into park. She went straight to the man standing off to the side, but he looked terrifying and filled the clearing with such a heaviness, it was hard to hold his gaze.

She looked at the ground, dragging air into her lungs, and held out her hand. "I'm Hallie," she rushed out before the words got clogged in her throat.

"You're human," a blonde woman said from where they all stood at the firepit.

She swallowed hard and offered her hand closer

to the man. "Hallie Carter. It's nice to meet you."

The man's hard eyes drifted from her face to her hand, then to something behind her. From the sound of the steadily approaching growl, she would guess Gunner was at her back.

"Lucas," the man said in a deep, gruff voice. He shook her hand and released it fast, twitched his head toward Gunner. "You'll save a fight if you go stand closer to him."

She didn't understand. "What do you mean?"

"Hallie," Gunner rumbled.

When she turned around, Gunner's face looked so strange in the flickering firelight. Every angle was too sharp.

The other two men slowly drifted over toward Lucas, eyes on Gunner.

Hallie blew out a shaking breath as she padded carefully over to Gunner. He stood rigid as a board. "Lucia—"

"I'll take care of her," a dark-haired beauty said from right beside Hallie. She startled hard, but the woman didn't seem to mind.

"Lucia," Lucas said, warning drenching his tone.

"What are you doing?" a blond-haired man with

glowing silver eyes asked the raven-haired beauty.

"I'm protecting a human from your pissing contest," she said, her voice cracking with power. "If you dumbasses start fighting, you don't pay enough attention to the collateral damage."

God, the air was hard to breathe.

"What are you doing here?" Lucas asked. "Back to burn the rest of it down? We just got the place rebuilt." He gestured to the four matching trailers behind him. "Life is going well, so what…you're here to fuck everything up again?"

"You can't come back here," the blonde-haired woman said. "You aren't a Warlander anymore." She twitched her head toward the woman still standing beside Hallie. "Lucia is the only one who feels anything kind for you, Gunner."

Movement beside her drew Hallie's attention down to Gunner's hand. He had balled it into a tight fist, but other than that, he didn't move a muscle.

"Please leave," the dark-haired man near Lucas growled. "Don't come back here anymore."

Gunner dropped his chin to his chest. He closed his eyes tightly and winced as if he was in pain. "I want to fight all of you," he growled.

"And that's why we need you to leave," Lucas said.

Gunner looked up at him. "I want to fight all of you, but it isn't personal. My animal just...Fuck." He inhaled deeply and let the breath out slowly. "I didn't know if I could do a Crew, and it was stupid to try. I'm not good at it. Not now. I know I fucked everything up. I know." Gunner's eyes were filled with emotion as he nodded at Lucas. "It's what I do. Not just now, but since we were kids. Since..." He gestured to the blonde woman. "Ever since Cadence. I don't remember everything—"

Lucas huffed a humorless sound and turned around, shaking his head.

"It's not an excuse, and I'm not here to make excuses," Gunner said. "I'm not asking to come back. I don't want to, even if you let me. I would just fuck it all up again. I just need closure."

"For your benefit. Closure not granted, you fuckin' asshole," Lucas growled.

Gunner glanced at Hallie, and then back at the Warlanders. "I don't need you to say you forgive me, but believe me, you can't punish me more than I punish me. I have these stupid flashbacks. It's the worst moments of the things I've done. The times I've fought you all. The blood I've drawn, the sounds of pain. The fire." He dropped his gaze to the ground again. "I wish you would've put me down," he whispered.

Gunner's jaw was clenched after that admission. Hallie slipped her hand into his and squeezed. Fuck. What a heartbreaking admission. Her eyes were burning with tears. She could tell Gunner really felt something deep for these people, but it was beyond her grasp what separating from a Crew meant. Was it like losing a family?

He swallowed hard. "I don't need your forgiveness. I just needed you to hear the truth in my voice when I tell you…I'm sorry." Gunner lifted his gaze to Lucas, and his voice dipped to a whisper. "I'm so fuckin' sorry. For everything. You were trying to help me, and I burned you for it." He made a clicking sound behind his teeth and tugged at Hallie's hand. "The park looks good. Things will be easier for you now."

He led Hallie back toward his truck, which still sat idling with the lights on.

"It was nice to meet you all," she said over her

shoulder. Her heart hurt so badly, but she didn't understand why. It was as if she was feeling Gunner's emotions or something.

This wasn't her story, but she felt a part of it now.

Gunner opened her door for her, waited for her to climb in before he shut the door, then strode around the front of the truck.

She watched the others talking by the firepit, and she imagined how much that had to hurt Gunner. He used to be a part of this, right? He was part of a tight-knit group of friends? And now he was on the outside.

It had been heartbreaking to watch, but she was really proud of him.

Gunner opened up his door to get in, but a loud, booming word echoed through the clearing. "Wait."

Gunner jerked his attention to Lucas, who was striding toward him.

A growl rattled Gunner's chest as he stepped out from behind the open door. "What?"

Lucas came to a stop in the bright beams of the headlights. He cast a glance back at the others, who seemed to be waiting. His broad shoulders lifted with his inhalation. "Look, I don't forgive you…" Lucas hung his head and shook it, hooked his hands on his hips. "You and your lady, come get a beer." Lucas turned and strode back to the firepit. Gunner just stood there frozen with this look on his face that was half wanting to run, half hope.

"I'm thirsty," she said quickly before he could hop into the truck and zoom them back toward Laramie.

Gunner glanced at her, and back to the Warlanders. Slowly, he leaned inside, turned the truck off, pocketed the keys, and made his way around to her door. When he'd helped her out, she snuggled tighter into her hoodie and walked beside him toward the firepit.

This introduction was different. Now, the Warlanders lined up and introduced themselves. Cadence, Jenna, Lucia, Landon, Kru, Lucas. The last one was Lucas. He reintroduced himself as Alpha of the Warlanders while Landon pulled a couple extra chairs up to the fire.

Cadence and Jenna showed her an old blue cooler of iced-down beer, and she got one for herself and one for Gunner before she settled into a chair between Lucia and Cadence.

"You're really human," Cadence said softly as the men all stood around talking on the other side of the firepit.

"Unfortunately, yes. I have no superpowers," she joked.

"It's not all it's cracked up to be for some of us," Lucia muttered.

"Gunner has said very nice things about you," she said to Lucia.

"Bet he didn't say anything nice about me," Cadence said.

"He told me about when you were kids, but he didn't say anything bad about you. He takes the blame."

Cadence frowned and fidgeted with the tab of her beer can. "He's told you a lot then."

"It's safe with me," Hallie assured her.

"Truth," Jenna said. "I'm gonna say it."

"Jenna," Cadence said.

"What? We're all thinking it."

"Say what?" Hallie asked.

"Well, we all just figured if Gunner ended up dating someone, she would have to be like a dragon or something."

"Or a hellhound," Cadence added.

"I'm also surprised you are human," Lucia said.

"Oh, we aren't dating. I just met him."

"Then why do you smell like him?" Lucia asked.

Hallie's eyes went wide. She didn't know how to explain that one away because they had definitely just boned in his motel room before they drove here, and she had the video of it sitting in her phone. "Sooo you have very good senses of smell," she said with a nervous laugh.

"No offense, but Gunner is rough. And you're..." Jenna let the words die off.

"Fragile? Agree, but I have a Taser."

Lucia snorted.

"Yeah, ask her how long it took her to use the damn Taser on me after she met me," Gunner said across the fire.

Hallie pursed her lips against a smile.

"You tased Gunner?" Cadence asked, then laughed so loud it echoed through the clearing.

Jenna and Lucia were throwing out questions over each other, big grins on their faces. "How long did you know him?"

"Four minutes?" she asked him across the fire.

"Maybe three," Gunner said, a smile tugging at his lips.

"In my defense, I was trying to keep him from killing someone. There were cameras around."

"In my defense, she tased me directly after I got shot," Gunner pointed out.

Hallie nearly spit out the beer she was drinking. With a gulp, and trying to contain her laugh, she said, "Okay, that sounds way worse than it was. The gunshot wasn't even near a vital organ."

"It broke my bone," Gunner muttered, lifting the sleeve of his T-shirt.

Landon leaned in and looked at it. "And it healed badly. Did you even clean it?"

"I went grizzly afterward. I didn't clean shit. I was trying to stop myself from going back to the gas station."

"I got the cashier to delete the camera footage," Hallie bragged. "I might have tased him, but I had his back."

Lucia asked Kru, "What are you doing?"

Kru was messing around on his phone. "Ordering us all Tasers."

The good-natured laughter that filled in the gaps of the conversations that followed settled something inside of Hallie. Seeing them all relax around Gunner was special. Seeing him relax felt even bigger.

She didn't know all of his story, or the story of his people. Not all of it, and not by a long shot, but she did feel a shift here tonight. She liked the girls. They were easygoing, and all very different. Jenna was quiet, but funny with one-liners. Cadence was the most outgoing, and she and her mate...mate? That's what they were called, right? She and Kru were very cute with how they talked to and orbited around each other. She might have been Gunner's first love, but there was nothing like that there anymore. Hallie could feel it. Lucia was the quietest, but she sat right beside Hallie all night, making sure she was drawn into any conversations, making sure she was included. She seemed very sensitive to other people, and Hallie appreciated it. She could also roast the boys like no other. That part was hilarious.

All four of those men were dominant. She didn't know their animals, other than Gunner's bear, but she suspected they were all predator shifters. They were very funny, but she had no doubt they could turn scary quick.

Badasses. She liked them very much.

Her favorite part of the night though...her very

favorite part…was the number of times she caught Gunner watching her. Eventually, the boys had sat back down at the firepit. Gunner had asked Lucia to scoot over a chair so he could sit by Hallie, and it made her feel special and seen and cared for. She liked that he sought closeness.

"It's pretty cool," Kru said, and then took a swig of his beer, eyes on Gunner.

"What is?" Cadence asked.

"Seeing Gunner not cussing us up and down."

"It'll come back," Gunner assured him.

Landon snorted. "The break is nice though."

"I made things fun around here," Gunner joked.

"You set our houses on fire," Jenna pointed out.

"Never a dull moment though," Gunner quipped.

Landon took a drink and settled in the big chair behind Lucia. "I hardly have to stitch anyone up anymore."

Kru mouthed, *Bullshit.*

Cadence said, "Yeah, you and Lucas bled each other like four days ago. Nice try."

Hallie drew her knees up. Even with the fire, the breeze chilled her a bit. Gunner saw the movement. "Let me go see if I have an extra hoodie in my truck."

He moved to stand up, but Cadence waved him down. "There's extra blankets in ten-ten."

She started to walk toward the single-wide trailer on the left, but stopped midway and turned with the strangest expression on her face. She locked eyes with Lucia. When Hallie looked at Lucia, the raven-haired woman wore a knowing smile.

Without breaking her gaze on Lucia, Cadence asked, "Hey Hallie, do you want a tour of ten-ten?"

"What's a ten-ten?" she asked.

"You'll see," Jenna murmured softly.

"Umm, sure." Hallie stood and looked to Gunner, but he wasn't angry at her leaving without his permission. He wasn't asking what she was doing, or asking her to mind rules she didn't understand. She swallowed down the instinct to ask him if it would be okay to go with Cadence.

He rocked up off the back of his chair and grabbed her ass as she leaned down and kissed him. "Have fun," he murmured as he relaxed back into the chair.

The flapping in her stomach didn't feel like butterflies anymore. It felt like dragons.

"I like your falcon tattoo," Jenna said as Hallie

walked past her.

She rarely thought of the big tattoo she'd gotten on the back of her leg, because she didn't see it back there much.

"Thanks," she told her.

"What's it mean?"

"It's a bird in flight, not perched. She's on a journey."

An easy smile stretched across Jenna's face and she nodded once, then lifted her drink to Hallie. Hallie tinked her can against Jenna's and followed Cadence to the cream-colored trailer with forest-green shutters.

She'd never actually been in a mobile home, so she didn't know what she'd expected, but when Cadence led her inside this one, she paused in the entryway and was filled with such....such...Hallie frowned, trying to understand herself.

"It happens to everyone," Cadence said. "Come on."

The dark laminate floors were a little soft to walk on, and some of the ceiling tiles were sagging in places. She saw a couple of mouse droppings on the floor, but the kitchen was cute. It was all white cabinets and wood-block counters. The living room was small but homey, with worn green couches and a little rug under a coffee table.

"Is this where you and Kru live?" Hallie asked as Cadence led her down a short hallway to a bedroom that didn't have any furniture in it, save a hope chest near the window.

Cadence knelt down, opened the top of the chest, and dug through a stack of blankets. "No one lives in this one right now."

"Ooooh. Was it Gunner's?" she asked quietly.

Cadence shook her head and pulled out a blanket, closed the lid, and sat on the chest. "Probably it should've been Gunner's. Maybe it would've made things easier for him."

She didn't understand. Hallie shook her head. "What do you mean?"

Cadence inhaled deeply and looked around the empty bedroom. "The legend of ten-ten is pretty big in these mountains."

"Oh." Hallie frowned, trying to catch up. "Well, it's very lucky that you have it in your trailer park then."

Cadence's slow smile was confusing. She stood and handed Hallie the blanket. "Luckier than you even know. Come on. Let's go make sure the boys aren't fighting. You are probably the only thing keeping Gunner's instincts under control right now."

"His instincts?"

Cadence turned and walked backward a few paces as she said, "This is the longest I've ever seen him go without ruining a night." She winked and turned back around, walked straight through the living room and out the front door, leaving Hallie to stare after her and wonder about Gunner's demons.

She looked around the cozy trailer and smiled to herself. Someday, she dreamed of being able to settle down someplace after Derek grew weary of chasing her and moved on. The old her would've wanted some big penthouse somewhere, but the new her? The humbled her? The her that breathed for peaceful, quiet moments, wouldn't mind having a place like this.

Boldly, she sank down on the edge of a couch cushion just to test out if it was as comfy as it looked. It totally was.

She would never say it out loud, because dreaming was pointless for a hunted girl like her, but in her most quiet moments from here on out, she would think of this place. This was the dream. It had everything she needed. Cute kitchen, homey feel, television mounted on the wall to cuddle up on the couch and eat popcorn and have movie marathons. Comfortable bedroom, and a cute bathroom. No dishwasher, but that was okay. She didn't mind handwashing dishes.

The door opened and she jumped, startled out of her daydream.

Gunner poked his head in. "We've got a long drive back," he murmured. "I can excuse us."

Hallie hugged the blanket closer to her chest. "I like it here."

Gunner looked around the room, and his face softened. He pulled up his phone and told her to, "Smile."

She struck a pose on that old green couch and cheesed as big as her lips would stretch. He poked a few buttons, and then shoved his phone into his back pocket and strode inside.

Her phone vibrated, and she checked the image he'd just texted her. She was struck by her own smile. For a few moments, she couldn't speak. She could only look at herself.

If her counselor saw this, she would point out that smile.

Gunner was watching her face, hands shoved deep into his pockets.

"I feel happy," she whispered thickly.

"Say more," he murmured.

She shrugged her shoulders up to her ears. "I like these people, and I like that they're badasses. I like that they're welcoming and warm, and I like their homes here, and I like…I like…"

"Go on."

"I like being around you and learning about your life. The good and the bad."

"Stay one more day." He repeated the same words he had said last night.

"And then what?" she answered, repeating the words she had responded with the night before.

"And then we'll see."

TWELVE

Hallie shut the door to Corey's house and pressed her back against it. She closed her eyes and smiled.

Gunner had taken her to pick up her car, and then followed her all the way to the entrance of Corey's property to make sure she got home safe.

Her phone lit up with a text. A part of her expected him to text her that she needed to update him whenever she got somewhere she intended to be, but it wasn't forceful. He just said, *I had fun today.*

A grin confiscated her face as she texted back, *Dinner after my shift tomorrow? It's payday. I'm buying.* Send.

Whooo girl, you taking me out?

She laughed. Hallie liked this. He wasn't fighting

her meager offerings like Derek used to do. Derek had wanted that control of having something to hold over her head.

I'm taking you out, and if you're real good I might even spring for dessert. There's this pie place I found in Laramie that's to die for.

Deal. We may have to push it back to a little later though. I have an appointment at four.

An appointment? So mysterious. Well good, that will give me a chance to come back to Corey's and change before dinner.

Wear booty shorts.

She snickered. *My ex hated when I wore those in public.* Send.

Fuck that dude. Cut them shorter.

She belted out a laugh.

Before she could reply, another text from Gunner came through. *I'm not trying to be mysterious, just didn't want to jinx it. Job interview.*

She let off a little gasp. *No jinxing it. Just tell me how it goes at dinner.*

Don't be upset if I don't get it. Long shot.

You will get laid either way. Send.

Oh fuck. A three-second video came through of

him in his dimly-lit truck. He had his eyebrows arched at the camera. He looked so handsome, glowing eyes and all.

Are you texting and driving? Send.

Hell no. A picture of the for-sale sign at the end of the gravel drive came through. *Making sure you got to the house safe, and then I got stuck still wanting to talk to you. I'm driving back to the motel now. Sleep like a log, pretty girl. And thank you.*

For what? Send.

For pushing me to apologize. Tonight was good.

She hugged the blanket that Cadence had insisted she keep tighter to her chest, and read that last text three times.

That man was something else. *Drive safe.* Send.

"That's a love-smile," Corey said.

Hallie yelped and dropped her phone, startled by her cousin's presence.

Corey was leaning against the wall at the mouth of the hallway, arms crossed. She looked tired.

"Hey!" Hallie greeted her. "What are you doing up?"

"Can't sleep," she said, sitting at the table. There was a stack of mail, and she pushed it toward the empty spot at the table. "You got something."

With a frown of confusion, Hallie sat down at the table and set the blanket next to her, then pulled the letter on top up so she could read the return address.

There wasn't one, but she recognized the handwriting on the address. Her heart dropped to the floor, and she whispered, "What the fuck?"

Corey looked haunted. "He sent the rest of these to my office over the past couple of days."

"Why didn't you tell me?" she asked, sifting through the letters. All were the same—no return address.

"You seemed happy and hopeful, and I thought he would send one or two and then let up. These four arrived today, and there was one in the mailbox."

"He's a psychopath," Hallie said, her blood chilling.

"I didn't really understand that until now," Corey admitted. "This is scary, Hallie."

She swallowed audibly and opened the top letter. Inside was a folded piece of computer paper. She unfolded it and read the words on the page.

Hallie, I miss you. I think you've mistaken my

intentions. I want to make you my wife. I gave up everything for you.

I'll never give up on us.

There was no name signed, but it was from Derek.

Her breath shook as she opened the next one.

I think about you all the time. You keep blocking me, but you don't understand. I want to take care of you. I want to have babies with you.

The next letter said:

Hallie. Please come home. I'm wasted without you. My family is all worried. Our family is worried. I'm not okay. Unblock me.

The next:

Why don't you update your Instagram page? You aren't scared of me. I know you aren't. I'm the only one who really knows you. I know what you want.

Hallie, please.

That one was written on his office letterhead. Sloppy, Derek.

Was he drunk when he wrote these?

She opened the next.

Hallie, I need to see you. I need to be inside of you.

Tears burned her eyes, and she crumpled up the last letter. Stunned, she stared out the window. "He will never stop," she said, angry.

Corey had pulled the open letters to herself, and looked horrified at reading them. "We need to take these to the police."

"They already told me they can't do anything about stalkers unless he does something physically harming to me."

"He broke your fucking nose."

"And I didn't go to the police about it then."

"Hallie, he knows where we live."

"I'll fix it."

"How? By running? That's not working."

"This isn't your problem."

"It is my problem! It's my problem!" Corey's cheeks were red with anger. "You are my family, Hallie." She held up the letters. "This guy is a crazy person. It's too much. Too heavy. You can't ignore these."

"I'm not ignoring them."

"Let's just go to the police," Corey pleaded.

Hallie dashed her hand across her damp cheeks. The awful feeling was back. The darkness was back, and she hated it. She looked down at the blanket she'd gotten from that little mobile home up in Damon's Mountains, and she wished things were different.

"Hey," Corey said, reaching across the table to squeeze her hand. "Have you asked him yet?"

"Asked who, what?"

"Asked Gunner to bite you?"

"To...bite me?" she asked, baffled. "What are you talking about?"

"We had a plan, remember? You can just pay him for the bite, and then you'll be safe. You'll be invincible. Derek can't touch you if you're a shifter. No one can."

"That's..." She winced and shook her head. "That's

not the plan."

"You have twenty-thousand dollars."

"Corey! Stop!"

"Gunner likes you, right? A bite is easy. I've been looking it up on the internet. He just has to bite you, and then you'll turn into a bear whenever you want to."

She was so shocked, Hallie just stared blankly at her cousin. That wasn't why she was spending time with Gunner. He wasn't some part of a plot, but this conversation made her feel gross.

"I like Gunner enough to never ask him to do that," she murmured, standing.

"Hallie, I'm scared." Corey lifted the letters in her fist. "This is terrifying."

"I'll take them to police tomorrow, and I'll order some cameras for the house tonight."

"So we can have a thirty-second warning before your ex skins us?" Corey asked.

But Corey didn't need to be scared. Hallie was already one foot out the door. This wasn't her problem, or Gunner's problem. Hopefully someday she would be able to come back here and find happy moments again, but the timing was wrong now. She sighed patiently and gathered the letters. "I'm going to the police station before my shift in the morning. You don't have to worry. I'll fix everything."

Corey sat back in her seat, eyes boring into Hallie. "I'm sorry this is happening."

Hallie loved her cousin so much. *So* much. She shrugged and forced a smile. "It's just another day in the life. I'll fix it."

She was glad Corey wasn't a shifter who could hear lies, but from the pursed-lip stare Corey offered her, she thought her cousin might just hear the lie in her tone anyway.

Hallie strode for her and hugged her tight. "I love you, cuz."

Corey clung to her, hugging her tightly. "I love you too. Police station first thing. Want me to come with you?"

"No, you have work, but I promise I'll go. I'll send you a selfie from the station so you know I'm following through."

"Good. Post that shit to your social media that he's so worried about. Maybe crazy-pants will get the hint that he could actually get arrested and leave you the fuck alone."

"I will," she promised, but she knew in her heart that wouldn't deter Derek. Nothing would. She was his greatest hunt. He would never stop until he was dead. Hallie was the first person who had ever told him no, and he wouldn't let it rest.

Hallie kept the forced smile plastered to her lips as she told her cousin goodnight, and all the way to the bathroom, and all the way through washing her face and brushing her teeth. A smile with tears in her eyes, because she was already plotting and planning. Her suitcase was still packed in her bedroom closet.

She forced the smile until she closed the bedroom door behind herself, locked it, and lay on the bed. She only let it slip as she stared up at the slowly-spinning ceiling fan.

Only then did she allow herself to fall apart.

She was happy here. Derek ruined everything.

****

Gunner squinted at the glowing phone screen. The text had come through in the middle of the night, but he'd had the phone on silent.

Sebastian Kane, the ID read. *Something's*

happening.

Bash?

In the dark before dawn, Gunner sat up in the motel bed and opened the text. *What's up?* Send.

Here is Derek Forester's social media page. Pay attention to the last three posts. There was a link to click, and Gunner hit it.

The page was pictures of some unfamiliar man with black hair and dark eyebrows. Clean-shaven, chiseled jaw, boring-ass looking model of a man. Dark eyes and an empty smile, and as he scrolled down, most of the pictures had a woman in them. Hallie. Holy fuck.

He threw the covers off his legs as his body overheated. He sat on the edge of the mattress, elbows on his knees as he scrolled down the page.

Tell me when you're done looking at his page, Bash texted.

Gunner flicked his text out of the way, and then scrolled to the beginning of his pictures with Hallie.

She was genuinely smiling in these. Happy, perhaps. There were pictures of her serving tables—smiling at him, waving, dressed in black pants and a white button-up shirt with an apron, her hair pulled back. It was bleach-blonde in these.

A picture of her sitting at a bar top, filling out paperwork.

A picture of them smiling in a selfie at some bar.

A snarl rattled his throat, and he ran his hand roughly through his hair. He didn't like any of this.

God, she was pretty, but as he scrolled up, her smile changed. There was a picture of them at some sort of black-tie event. She was wearing a skintight, sequined black dress. She looked gorgeous, but her eyes were empty as she smiled at the camera. Derek was whispering in her ear. To anyone else it might've seemed like a romantic picture, but Gunner knew her real smile. This wasn't it.

There were more selfies of her walking behind him, her head down, her eyes vacant. Her nose was perfect, and then it wasn't. Then it was crooked. He checked the dates of those posts. There was a six-week gap, probably to let her heal up.

The snarl got louder and he stood, hoping to relieve the tingling in his fingers.

Her eyes went completely blank in the pictures following. There were thousands of likes on these posts. Thousands and thousands. His captions were quirky and quick-witted, explained away her disassociation with little jokes.

...One of us hates pictures more than the other...

...I thought it was the woman who would want to ask for selfies...

...deep down she loves me...

She wasn't happy in any of these pictures.

There were hundreds of comments talking about how gorgeous she was, asking when he would propose to her, encouraging him to have beautiful babies with her.

He wanted to puke.

One comment on a picture of her vacant stare caught his attention. *She looks miserable.* The comment had been posted by a Corey Gable. That was her cousin. He just knew it. Attagirl.

He scrolled up through beautiful empty-eye pictures of her shopping with him, of him buying her a car, handing her a key to a gorgeous apartment.

He scrolled up and up to the last three posts, like Bash had pointed out.

A few days ago, Derek had posted a picture of a glass of liquor on ice in some fancy bar with high-end bottles in the background. *Missing my lady. Do you think I should go get her back?*

Thousands of likes.

Hundreds of comments encouraging him to do it.

The next one was a picture of him in a boardroom, arms locked on a table, talking to a room full of people. *Another day in the office. All the money in the world doesn't mean shit if I'm going home to an empty house. God, I miss her.*

Thousands of likes.

Hundreds of comments telling him to go get her.

The last post was from yesterday. It was just a picture of Hallie sleeping in some ritzy apartment. *Going on a trip. Be back soon. This house is too empty without her.*

Gunner set the phone beside him on the bed, squeezed his hands onto his thighs, and stared at the table beside his bed.

He blew a steadying breath out. One. Two. Three breaths.

I'm done looking at his page, Gunner texted Bash.

Okay. Now look at this. There was another link.

Gunner clicked it. Hallie's page came up. It only had six posts on it, total.

Two of them were older, of her when her hair

was bleach-blonde, but the last four he understood. Why? Because he was in three of the posts, and he'd taken the picture for the other one.

With a frown, Gunner clicked on the picture of him smiling across the table at that bar after she'd fallen apart in counseling. He was leaning on the table, looking out the window, hand on the empty shot glass, a smile on his face. The caption read, *The only thing I'm interested in these days.*

Huh. He would've been flattered if she hadn't posted this in the middle of the night and tagged Derek in it. This was shots-fired at Derek, and he was being used to do it.

He scrolled to the next one. It was the picture he'd taken of her in ten-ten. She was smiling so big. *Finally happy. Happy to leave my past behind.*

Shot. Fired. Three hours ago.

The next was the video Corey must've sent her of Hallie getting on the back of his motorcycle, then them speeding off into the night. *His*, the caption read.

The final post was a video. She'd taken it when they were driving and singing to a Slipknot song. *Finally, someone who gets me and doesn't shatter my*

FUCKING FACE. In the video she was smiling so big and dancing in the passenger's seat of his truck. The video was shaky as she aimed it at him. He had an arm draped over the steering wheel, and an easy smile he didn't even recognize on himself. He was singing the song word-for-word with her. There were three dots under the picture that meant there were more pictures to this post. He scrolled to the next, and it was a picture of her with bleach-blonde hair, aiming the camera at the mirror—her nose bashed, blood pouring down her chin, her eyes swollen from crying and empty.

Fuck. FUCK!

The next picture was a video of her sobbing on the floor of a bathroom with bruises on her swollen face.

She'd tagged Derek Forester in the post.

Chest heaving with fury, Gunner requested to tag himself in the post. He'd posted exactly zero pictures on this account. He'd set it up years ago and never done anything, but now? He posted the picture he had of Hallie in ten-ten and captioned it, *Yep. Mine.*

And then he went and changed his bio tagline. *Derek Forester: we have business. Gunner Walker, bear shifter, Damon's Mountains. You better not show up anywhere near Hallie. You better fucking hide.*

He closed out of his social media and texted Hallie, *You okay????* Send.

He paced the room as he waited for her to respond, but minutes passed with nothing.

Shit. Shit! She'd called out her abuser. She'd called out her stalker. She'd used Gunner to do it, knowing that would just agitate a psycho like Derek. Something had set her off, but what?

Hallie, what happened?? Send.

He checked his phone again, but there was nothing except a text from Bash. *Stop her.*

Fuck!

Gunner pulled on a T-shirt and jeans, shoved his wallet in his back pocket, grabbed the keys to his motorcycle, and rushed out the door. He clicked his phone onto the mount on his bike and checked his gas, then ripped out of the parking lot and aimed his motorcycle for her cousin's house.

He rode like hell, barely slowing for the turns until he was throwing gravel behind his back tire as he ruined the gravel on the way up to Corey's house. He'd never been all the way up, but he barely stopped and shoved the kickstand down before he was running to the front door.

He didn't miss it.

Hallie's car wasn't here.

He knocked. Knocked again.

Looked in the front window, but the blinds were drawn.

He knocked again and shoved his visor up.

"Hang on!" came a yell from inside.

Corey yanked open the door, and Gunner was met with a handgun to his face. "Good," he barked. "Where's Hallie?"

Corey frowned. "What?"

"Where is she?"

She rubbed her sleepy eyes and glanced around the living room. "Probably still asleep. It's an atrocious hour."

"Her car isn't here," he rumbled, pushing past her.

"You can't just come in here uninvited."

"I'm not a fucking vampire." He followed Hallie's scent to a bedroom in the back, but she wasn't there. "When did she leave?"

"I—I don't know," Corey murmured. Truth. "She was upset last night. She's going to the police station to...turn...in..." Corey's wide eyes were on a stack of papers on the nightstand in Hallie's room.

Gunner pulled them up and quickly read through them. Shhhhhit. These were what happened. This was the reason for her posts.

"Maybe she just forgot those?" Corey said. Her tone was frantic. "She's probably at the police station."

"Check her social media," he growled. "Would she fly to him, or drive?"

"I..." Corey shook her head and blinked hard.

"Fly or drive?" he asked.

"I don't know."

"Corey," he growled, gripping her shoulders. "I'm going to help her, but I need to know where to go."

"Okay, wait, wait, wait," she yelled, running for another bedroom. She picked up her phone and poked a few buttons, read over something—probably the posts Hallie had made in the middle of the night. "Oh my gosh, she's going after him."

"Yep, now you're all caught up. How? How would she do it?"

"Fuck, fuck, fuck, let me think," Corcy said, burying her face in her hands. "Is there a tracker in her car? She said something about a tracker."

"I took it out and gave it to a friend, and he gave me Derek's information. From Derek's posts, he's heading here to find her."

"Oh my gosh. Okay. Okay!" Corey's hands were shaking, and she paced the room. "He will fly in a private jet. Hallie would unblock him, and text him an address to meet. She would never allow him to come to my house. She would make sure I was out of the way. She would protect me."

He could see her point. "Call her. See if she will pick up for you."

Corey connected a call and paced the room, chewing her thumbnail as she waited. "No answer."

Gunner tried, but no answer. Just voicemail. He texted her. *I want to be there. You aren't alone.*

There were dots like she was typing, and he was consumed with hope, but the dots stopped. He tried again. *I'm with you. I can help. Where are you?*

His text didn't go through.

"What does this mean?" he asked Corey, pointing to the white dot next to his text.

"She's blocked you."

"Fuck!"

"Let me try!" She texted, but yelled a curse and aimed her phone at him. Her text wasn't going through either.

He huffed a pissed-off laugh. He would've done the same thing. He wouldn't have wanted help.

Stubborn woman.

He connected a call to Bash.

"What do you need?" Sebastian Kane answered.

"She's not at her house. Left in the night, and she's blocked me and her cousin. Can you track her phone?"

"What's her number?"

As if she'd heard the conversation, Corey pointed her phone screen at Gunner. Hallie's number was pulled up, and he recited it to Bash.

"If you can find any other way to track her, do it. This takes time," Bash growled out. "I'll call when I have a location."

"Bash, can you track the person on the other side of that tracker you have?" Gunner asked, throwing a shot into the universe.

Bash got quiet for a few seconds. "You are good. Hallie is lucky." The phone clicked, and the line was dead.

What did that mean? Could Bash track the other end of the tracker, or not?

"What can I do?" Corey asked.

"Can you go to the police station and just make sure she's not there?"

"Yep!" And God bless that woman, she strode right for the front door, pajamas and messy hair and all. She snatched a set of keys off the hook by the door and disappeared outside. "Wait!" she yelped, appearing inside again as he reached the door. "I should maybe get your number so we can exchange information."

"Yep." He took her phone, entered his number as a new contact, and saved it. "Text me."

Hi, this is Corey.

He saved her number and nodded. "I'll let you know if I find out anything," he assured her.

"You know," she said. "If you would've just said yes, none of this would be happening."

Gunner didn't understand. "Say yes to what?"

"To her paying for you to Turn her. If she could turn into a bear right now, we wouldn't even have to help her. Twenty thousand is a lot of money. You should've just said yes." Corey offered him a quick half-smile and then jogged for her car, leaving him to stare after her in an awful shock.

Hallie had wanted to pay him to Turn her?

Hallie had wanted to pay for a bite?

From Gunner?

A sick, churning feeling took his middle.

Hallie had talked to her cousin about wanting to pay him for a bear? Twenty thousand? Dollars?

He couldn't move. He couldn't make his legs step forward.

Hallie...the woman he wanted...the woman he was falling for. She wanted to pay for his bite? That's why... He swallowed hard. That's why she was spending time with him?

Corey sped away in her car, and still, he stood there like an idiot, his brain completely shorted out.

Hallie had wanted to pay for a bite?

He was nothing but a means to a bite?

A flash of Cadence's face as she told him he was just a rebound washed across his mind.

His breath was pulled from his lungs as he saw the memory.

"I'm sorry, Gunner, you're just not it. I just wanted to get over him...you were just a way to get over him."

Gunner squatted and clenched his fists against the roaring in his ears, stared in horror at the cracked sidewalk as the memory of Cadence wrecking him played over again.

...you were just a way to get over him...

Hallie was different. Right? She was supposed to be different.

Lucia had made it seem like he was doing something good—like he was heading in the right direction, but was he?

Or was Hallie just another lesson?

THIRTEEN

Hallie balled her fists on her thighs to stop the shaking. She had been scared for so long, but that wasn't what was causing her trembling.

Now she was angry.

Her entire life had been in a chokehold.

How dare a man consume her life like this. How dare him.

She looked at the text thread again. Derek had landed at Laramie Regional Airport two hours ago on a red-eye flight, and he'd wanted to meet at a hotel nearby. She knew better than to meet a stalker at a hotel. She wanted something more public, so she'd agreed to meet him here. She lifted her gaze to the sign that read *Barker's World-Famous Breakfast*

Sandwiches.

She'd been here before and it had been slammed first thing in the morning, but today there were only a few groups eating at the picnic tables outside.

She'd gotten here early, but all that had served to do was give her time to count her regrets. There were so many.

After this, she would be free.

She would come back to her car, turn her notifications back on, and tell Gunner it was done. She would tell Corey it was over.

She just had to talk some sense into Derek and make him see that she didn't belong to him. She belonged to herself.

The sound of a fast-car engine filled the gravel parking lot, and she checked the side-view mirror to see a Ferrari pulling into the parking lot. Of course. She didn't even know where he would track down a rental company with Ferraris here. Then again, he could've stopped at a dealership and just bought the damn thing for fun. She'd seen him do way more frivolous things just for clout.

Bright side, he wouldn't be able to kidnap her. She could definitely fight being dragged into a small car like that. Especially this close to the police department. She lifted her attention to the department sign just two doors down. She'd chosen this place carefully.

The car revved as it parked one empty space away from her. She watched him get out, standing smoothly, pulling his designer sunglasses off his face. He wore gray slacks, a navy button-up shirt, and dress shoes. He was tall and chiseled and looked like some Ken doll come to life, only she knew how ugly he was on the inside.

Derek was a monster in disguise.

A trill of nervousness filled her stomach, and she steeled herself to greet him. Her door creaked open. He stood at the front of her car, hands buried in his pockets, watching her.

He had the smile of a snake.

"I don't know why you insist on driving this old rust-bucket around, Hallie. You know you can have any car you want."

"I like my car. I bought it myself."

The smile slipped from his lips and slowly returned, but she'd seen it—that flash of anger.

Chills rippled up her spine. "I have something I

want to say to you."

Derek inhaled sharply and looked around. "I would like to have breakfast with you."

"We don't have to do all the—"

"I have traveled a long way to be with you," he gritted out. "If we're going to have a serious conversation, the least you could do is eat with me one last time."

Stupid hope bloomed in her chest. Okay. Okay. So he was aware of what this was. This was the last time. This was the goodbye.

She nodded. "All right."

She walked beside him, out of arm's reach. He cast her a glance. "You look pretty. At least I think you do. Your sunglasses don't suit your face, love. They're too big. They cover too much of your bone structure."

She would've worn one of Gunner's hoodies with the hood up if she wasn't sweating with nerves right now. She hated the way Derek looked at her.

"It's cloudy out," he said. "Why don't you take those off so I can see your eyes."

"I'm comfortable the way I am."

"Clearly. Your shorts get more provocative every time we see each other. Is that for me?"

She patted her purse just to feel the weight of the Taser inside of it. That settled her. "Yep, I wear the clothes I know you hate, so I guess you could say it's for you. Kind of like a middle finger, Derek."

Beside her, he shook his head, and gestured for her to sit at a picnic table. She didn't really like having her back to her car, but he took a seat across from her and some battles were not worth it.

"Relax," he murmured, gesturing for her to take her cross-body purse off.

She gritted her teeth and reached for the plastic menus that sat at the edge of the table by the salt and pepper and a red ketchup bottle.

Derek reached it first. "Let me." He handed it to her, and part of her wanted to refuse it. She didn't want him thinking she was accepting a kindness. "I already know what I want." *To fuckin' leave.*

His jaw twitched with how hard he clenched his teeth, and then he pulled the offered menu to himself. "I don't know why you insist on arguing. I'm not here to argue. I just want things to go back to the way they were."

"How were they, Derek?" she asked, crossing her arms on the table.

"You remember." He gestured to her messy bun. "Your hair is much too pretty to wear it like that. I shouldn't say that, I know, but you should hear the compliment in it. You know me."

"Snide remarks and passive-aggressive insults aren't compliments."

His fingers tightened on the menu, and he leaned forward. There it was, the rage in his eyes. He parted his lips to say something, but was interrupted by the waitress.

"Hi folks! What can I get you to drink?"

Derek clacked his mouth closed and then leaned back, relaxed. He offered his charming-snake smile to the waitress. "I'll have an Old Fashioned."

The woman laughed, but the sound died in her throat as she realized he was serious. "It's not even seven in the morning."

"We're celebrating an anniversary," he said softly.

"Oh, congratulations. Ummm, we don't serve alcohol here though."

He inhaled slowly, his nostrils flaring with his irritation. "Fine, I'll have sparkling water then."

"Um, bad news—"

"Let me guess. You don't serve sparkling water

either. Bottled water will do."

"We only have tap water."

"I'll just have whatever it is the locals drink," he gritted out.

"I'll have orange juice," Hallie said brightly. "Feel free to spit in his drink."

The woman's mouth fell open.

"I'm being serious. I apologize for his atrocious manners. He's not from around here."

"Right. Do you know what you would like to eat?"

"She will have the country breakfast sandwich, the egg over-medium with no salt or pepper, and do you have Swiss cheese?" he asked. "My wife has a preference."

His wife? She was stunned into silence, and glared at him the entire time he ordered his meal.

"Your wife?" she asked as the waitress made her way inside.

"Close enough."

"We aren't married, so no, not close enough."

"You didn't say no when I put a three-carat ring on your finger."

"Oh, the one you gave me after you choked me in the bathroom at the Buckman's charity ball? That one?"

"Lower your voice."

"Fuck you, Derek. You didn't even ask me to marry you. You just put that ridiculous thing on my finger while I was asleep as yet another apology for you not being able to control your temper."

"Why are you so angry?" he asked low, leaning over the table. "You used to be fine with all of this."

"Fine with it? I was terrified. I was scared of doing anything wrong."

"Well, you were learning."

"Learning what?"

"How to behave as my wife and the mother of my future children. You think just anyone can join my family and take my last name? No. I lowered the bar to introduce you into my life, but there has to be compromise, the same as with any relationship. We have had shaky moments, yes, but I always care enough to make up for them. The good outweighs the bad."

"And money is what you consider the good."

He chuckled and scanned the parking lot. "It is the good."

"I am not your wife and I will never be your wife,

Derek. I will never be anything to you. I want nothing to do with you. No, stop laughing. Look at me." She shoved the sunglasses up onto her head and looked him dead in the eye. "I don't love you. I don't care about you. I don't even like you. In fact, sitting here looking at you gives me this awful, sick feeling in my stomach because you bring up all these memories I want to forget. I am not your anything."

"Stop," he said softly.

"I am not yours. I am not yours. I am *not yours*."

He twitched his head to the side and said it again. "Stop."

"I will never be yours—"

"Because of Gunner?" he asked suddenly. And ooooh, there was that familiar ice in his eyes. "Gunner Walker, bear shifter, the son of Haydan and Cassie Walker, raised in the Ashe Crew, owns a Ducati, net worth is fifty-thousand dollars. Total. Not suitable for pairing at this time. Stellar taste in men, Hallie. And while I do understand you were out in the world trying to discover yourself, slumming it isn't the way. You will have to regain my trust."

"Regain your trust? Fuck you. We aren't in a relationship. I ran away from my entire old life just to escape you. That's how much I wanted nothing to do with you. Gunner Walker listens to me, doesn't stalk me like a psychopath, is protective of me, and would not hurt me! Gunner Walker, net worth fifty thousand—value as a man, ten times what you could ever wish to be. And he's a demon in the sack. Lose my number, Derek. Stop hunting me. Stop sending people after me. Stop putting trackers in my car. Stop checking up on me, and stop sending me your pathetic letters—"

"Pathetic letters—"

"Yeah. Pathetic. If you have to stalk a woman just to track down an address to send your creepy notes to, it's pathetic."

He slammed his fist onto the table, and she lurched back, scared.

"Do you realize who you are talking to? Do you?" he yelled. "You are nothing. You are beneath me. You are a poorly-bred woman who lucked into good bone structure and a sex appeal that yes, does keep me interested. You have this fire that made me lower my standards and elevate you into a society you would've never even imagined if you hadn't tacked your life to mine. And then you leave with no warning—"

"Because you hurt me," she whispered.

"Because you fucking deserved it! You know you did. That's the real problem. You didn't like how much you were failing with me, and you don't do well with accountability. You ran because you are weak."

"Sir, I think you should stop talking to the lady like that," an older gentleman said from a couple tables down.

"Fuck you, you mangy inbred animal," Derek aimed at him.

This had been a bad idea. There was no progress.

"Why can't you just let me go?"

"Because you aren't allowed to leave me," he gritted out. "No one leaves me, and especially not someone like you."

"I think you should go," the waitress told him from where she stood a few yards back, holding their drinks. "This lady can stay, but you need to leave."

Behind her was a bigger man, likely the manager of the restaurant. "Leave, or we can see how long it takes the police to come pick your fancy ass up."

If Hallie wasn't trying to fight off a panic attack, she would've smiled in gratefulness to small towns who took care of their own.

She loved it here. She didn't know any of these people, but they were all standing and gathering loosely around their table.

Derek looked around at all of them and huffed a humorless laugh.

"You're a long way from home, Derek," she illuminated him. "No one here gives a rip who you are."

Derek's glare bore straight to her soul, and he nodded. There was something there…something evil in his eyes.

"See you real soon, Hallie," he murmured, then stood and strode for his Ferrari. He peeled out of the parking lot, spewing gravel onto all of them.

She sat there shaking until he disappeared down the main road away from the police department.

"Oh my gosh," she whispered in a trembling voice as the waitress's hand rested on her shoulder.

"Honey, are you okay?" she asked.

Her entire body was shaking with adrenaline, and perhaps trauma from the flashbacks that were so easily accessible when she was near that horrible man.

She reached into her purse, pushed the Taser aside, and dragged out her wallet.

"You don't have to worry about it," the waitress started.

"I want to. That wasn't fair for you to deal with either, and the kitchen is probably already making the food. I'm so sorry," she said, setting two twenties into her hand. "No one should treat any of us like that." She stood and started walking toward her car, flustered down to her bones. "Thank you for sticking up for me," she called to the people who were gathered around the restaurant.

New plan—the second she settled down, she needed to message Gunner and tell him what happened and what Derek had said. *See you real soon.* And he knew Gunner's information? Would he go after Gunner too? What about Corey?

She'd thought after a calm, civil talk, he would just go away when he saw she was different, and stronger, and out of his reach, but all it did was make things worse.

She got into her car and pulled past a black pickup that had parked way too freaking close to her passenger's side door. Swallowing down a sob, she pulled onto the main road.

She wanted to go straight to the motel and see Gunner. He probably wasn't even awake yet, but she just wanted to be in his arms and feel safe again. It was her day off work, so that was settled. She would go feel safe, and she and Gunner and Corey would come up with a good plan. Maybe going to the police again was the right direction. Maybe she could get some of the people at that restaurant as witnesses that he had come to her town—

Metal touched the side of her head, and she gasped and slammed on her brake.

"No, keep steady. Just drive."

A horrified glance in the rearview showed there was a familiar man in the back seat of her car. He was the guy from the gas station. The man with the shaggy brown hair and the scar on his lip. His face was swollen and bruised still from Gunner's fists, and his wrist was in a cast.

His dark eyes drilled into her, and he cocked the gun. "I wouldn't push it. Drive straight. I'll tell you where to turn."

Heaving panicked breath, she looked around and was terrified to see Derek's Ferrari waiting ahead on the side of the road. When she passed, he smoothly pulled behind her car.

"Why are you doing this?" she asked, and damn her voice for sounding so scared!

"Money."

"Whatever he's paying you, I can pay you more. I have twenty-thousand dollars in my savings. I can give it all to you. I can drive to the bank right now and withdraw it. You can have it, and I'll never talk about this to anyone."

"That would be a good offer if he wasn't paying me three times that. See that sign up ahead?"

"Y-yes."

"Turn left at it."

She didn't understand. It was a small neighborhood, and he had her circle the streets a few times before she pulled back out onto the main, where Derek's car was waiting across the road. He slid in behind her again, and they headed out.

"Why did I have to do that?" she asked.

"You fucked a shifter."

Her mind was racing. She should keep him talking! "So?"

"So, they are good trackers. I'm from these parts.

Been living in the shadows of Damon's Mountains all my life. I know how they work. Even if your little fuck-buddy found the restaurant and tracked the fumes, he will be stuck in that neighborhood for an hour. The scent will go cold on him. I'll take care of him later, after I'm paid. Mr. Forester said he would double my fee after I'm done with your shifter."

Oh my gosh, oh my gosh. Think!

She glanced at her purse. Her Taser and her cell phone were in there.

The man leaned through the gap between the seats and grabbed her purse, rifled through it, and held up her phone. "This what you wanted? Roll down the window."

"Please. I haven't done anything to you. Please just let me go."

"Roll down the window!"

She squeaked in fear and hit the window button for the back, but just by inches.

"Lower!" he yelled, ramming the barrel of the gun harder against her temple.

With a yelp, she rolled it down farther, and he chucked her phone out the window. It clattered onto a gravel turnoff.

The hopelessness that followed that moment was overwhelming. There was an awful empty feeling that consumed her as she gripped the steering wheel and coasted on the empty road. It was just after seven in the morning and there weren't many cars on the road.

He told her to take a right on a road that looked like nothing more than a washed-out, one-lane mud pit. Her car barely made it through the muck before she hit higher, more solid ground. Higher and higher they climbed until a small house came into view.

"Home sweet home," the man murmured. "Park the car and get out."

She cast a quick glance back to her purse in the back seat. The Taser was in there, if only she could get to it in time.

She unbuckled and bunched her muscles as the man got out of the car, but as she twisted around to grab her purse, the driver's side door opened and she was yanked out. She screamed at the pain in her arm, but Derek clapped his hand over her mouth. "Come on now, Hallie. That is beneath you."

She fought like some wild animal, but he reared back and hit her so hard, she fell to the ground on her hands and knees. The high-pitched ringing in her ears and the pain in her cheek made the edges of her vision blurry.

Derek grabbed the back of her hair and yanked her backward until she was looking up at the sky. He was saying something in her ear, but she couldn't understand his words.

Above her, in the sky, there was a falcon like the one in her tattoo. In flight, not perched. On a journey. This was a sign, right? This was God telling her to take heart? Or to disappear strong?

Tears stung her eyes.

The falcon was circling, and it screeched loud enough to reach Hallie's ears.

Derek yanked her upward and dragged her toward the house, but Hallie tried to keep her focus on the bird. It was the last beautiful thing she would see.

Oh, she knew what this was. Derek wouldn't be able to talk her into coming back in line in this house. He meant her harm. He was paying this man an insane amount of money to help him bring her harm.

Hallie struggled and got one last look at her car, parked sideways in the dirt driveway, before she was yanked inside.

The slamming of the door behind her was the loneliest sound in the world.

"Tie her to the chair," Derek said, gesturing to a ladder-back chair at the table. There was a huge window that overlooked a back deck, and Derek saw it at the same time she did.

There was a man on the back porch, his back to them, his hands in his pockets. He wore a black T-shirt and black jeans. He was looking toward the woods.

"Who the fuck is that?" Derek demanded.

The man who held her by the back of the neck had frozen. "I don't fuckin' know."

The man outside turned his face, and her heart kicked up to a gallop. She knew that face.

Hallie smiled. "You are in so much trouble."

Gunner turned and settled his glowing bi-colored eyes on them through the window, and then twitched his head. *Come here.*

"Is that one of those fucking shifters?" Derek asked.

"That's...that's..." The man looked terrified, and her smile grew wider at the memory of Gunner holding him up in the air with one hand.

"Gunner Walker," she murmured. She lifted her voice higher and repeated what Derek had said earlier. "Bear shifter, the son of Haydan and Cassie Walker, raised in the Ashe Crew—"

"Shut up!" Derek roared.

Gunner turned his entire body and lifted his chin, stared directly at Derek with the devil's smile painting his lips. "If you pull a trigger anywhere near her, I will pull every limb from your body. Slowly. No one will hear you scream."

Chills lifted up her spine. He meant it. She could tell.

"I didn't sign up for this," the guy beside her said.

"Get out there and shoot him."

The man was already backing away. "It was different when they weren't involved."

"Shoot him!" Derek ordered.

"Yeah, shoot me," Gunner called through the window. "Shoot me again, *Ben Snider*."

The gun clattered to the floor and the man held his hands up in surrender, backing toward the front door.

Hallie dove for the gun, but Derek was closer and

faster. He grabbed it and shoved her into the table, then launched at her. He grabbed her hair and put the barrel of the gun to her temple. "Move," he ordered, shoving her forward.

Breath coming in short bursts, she allowed him to move her forward through the back door and onto the deck.

Gunner's terrifying eyes tracked her, and then he turned toward the forest again as Derek maneuvered her ten feet away from him, facing the same direction.

"I'm going to kill you," Gunner promised him.

"I'll pull the trigger before you can get to her," Derek countered.

"I can tell you're not from around here. Clearly you have no idea what you stepped in the middle of."

An enormous silverback gorilla strode slowly through the trees on massive, powerful arms, his glowing gold eyes trained on Derek.

Lucas.

Chills, chills, chills.

The feline roar of something terrifying sounded through the woods. The falcon was circling above, and Gunner...Gunner was cool, calm, and collected.

"The police station is right down the road," Derek

murmured. "My family and all my followers know where I have come. Even if I disappear, they know where to look."

"Aaah. See, the police feel that they can't do anything until you've harmed Hallie. I don't have those constraints. And see that gorilla out there? His mother is the sheriff around here. I know exactly how this story will be spun." Gunner blinked slowly and then slid an empty gaze to Derek. "You posted about coming here after Hallie. You found her home. You sent your creepy fuckin' stalker letters. You harassed her cousin at her job. Hallie went to the police already, so they have the pictures of her battered face. They have the story. They know."

"I'll get locked up for a few months, then money will talk and I'll be out with my family before you know it, and you will still be worthless, and Hallie will still be a shifter's whore—"

Gunner blurred to them, and then the gun was gone. Simple as that. The metal was released from her temple and the click of weaponry sounded before three pieces of the gun hit the deck, and before she even registered anything, Gunner had thrown Derek against the big tree in the middle of the yard.

The silverback beat his fists on his chest, and now she could see a tiger slinking around the corner of the house.

She would've been terrified of the animals before, but not now. They were here to help her. To save her.

Derek was on his hands and knees, yelling in pain. Gunner was approaching him slowly, stalking forward, his hands in his pockets like they had never left, his head cocked. "You think you're above consequence, and that's why you got away with this for so long," Gunner told him.

"You can't just kill me," Derek gritted out.

"Why not?" Gunner asked, kneeling down in front of him. He shook his head, and Hallie could see how empty his gaze was from here.

Gunner could be terrifying.

"I probably won't even remember it," Gunner said. "Not unless the bear allows it. I won't have remorse. I won't feel guilt. No one will come for me."

"My family will come for you."

"Ooooh," Gunner warned. "You better hope they don't."

A man's scream echoed through the woods, and Gunner pointed to the sky. "You hear that? That's your help." Gunner leaned closer. "Did you pay him enough?"

Another death scream echoed through the woods, and then a grunt, and then silence.

"Ready?" Gunner asked.

Derek looked terrified there on his hands and knees. His eyes were so wide, and he was panting in fear.

"You shouldn't watch this," someone said from behind her. Lucia stood in the open doorway of the back door with a grim expression.

A roar sounded, and the wind kicked up to a hurricane. It flattened Hallie on the deck, and she struggled to look up into the sky. A massive darkness covered the dawn light, and she gasped in horror as an enormous blue dragon flew just above the tree line.

A stream of lava and fire spewed from his mouth into the woods, and a deafening roar sounded, shaking the trees.

"We gotta go," Lucia rushed out, dragging her backward by the arm. "We've gotta get out of here!"

But for the rest of her life, Hallie would never be able to banish the vision of Gunner's grizzly ripping out of him, or the dragon's fire engulfing the trees behind him. She would never forget the scars on the bear or the emptiness in his eyes, or the sound of Derek's last scream.

"Gunner!" she yelled as she was dragged into the house.

"He'll be okay! Damon knows he's here!"

Lucia pulled her by the hand out the front door and toward her car. Time slowed as fear consumed her. Each second was a minute as she ran for her life. Smoke was rolling across the yard, and the heat was blistering from the trees on fire.

"He's circling back," Lucia yelled. "Cadence, let's go!"

The white tiger was already running down the hill, and through the trees she could see something blurred and brown.

"Is that....is that a cougar?" she asked, gunning it on the straightaway.

"Saber-toothed tiger." Lucia pointed out the front window. "Watch out!"

A massive grizzly bolted in front of them and turned, running with them. The sky was getting darker by the moment.

"Is that Damon Daye?" she asked, terrified as she saw the monster in the rearview.

"Sure is, and out in broad daylight, which means he doesn't give a fuck who sees him burn these woods to ash."

"I don't feel right leaving Gunner!"

"Lucas has him."

"I don't feel right!" she yelled, hitting the brakes.

Lucia reached across the console and grabbed her face, jammed it toward the window. "Your man is there! Drive!"

The scarred, dark-furred grizzly was bolting down the hill through the trees, and the silverback was running on all fours farther into the trees.

Lucia shoved her leg down to hit the accelerator. "Go if you want to live!"

The dragon's wings were ripping smaller trees from the ground around them, and the car zoomed forward with the force of the wind as she gunned it. The back tires spun out at every curve in the road, and she looked at Lucia to see fear in her eyes as she held onto the dashboard, bracing for fire.

A stream of flames lit up the woods behind them.

"Why is he doing this?" she asked breathlessly.

"He's one of your people."

"His flames aren't for us," Lucia said grimly. "No one will ever find your abductors."

Wide-eyed, Hallie looked up at the rearview to see the dragon diving down from the sky. He scooped earth into his jaws and pulled up, ashes streaming from his mouth as he beat his massive wings against the wind currents.

Until this moment, she hadn't realized.

She hadn't known.

She'd never really understood why humans had talked about shifters with a quiet fear and reverence.

She cast a glance out her window to see Gunner easily keeping pace with her car, his ears back. He cast her an empty glance and kept running.

Now she understood.

Humans weren't the top of the food chain, like they tried to convince themselves they were.

Shifters were.

FOURTEEN

The others had left hours ago.

Hallie sat on the front porch of Corey's house with an oversized hoodie on, a glass of red wine next to her. She'd found her phone on the side of the road, and though the screen was cracked, she could still see if texts came through. Gunner still hadn't responded.

She didn't understand. Was he still a bear? Maybe he needed time in the woods. Or maybe they were having a meeting about what had happened. She wished she had the numbers of some of the Warlanders so she could ask.

Lucia had come back with her, and told her to hang low for a couple of days and stay out of town.

She'd watched the news footage of the blue

dragon burning the woods, but it was shaky cellphone footage from far away. It was lucky that no one had seen them all fleeing the mountain.

Damon had appeared in an interview an hour later with an explanation that his dragon sometimes needed to eat ashes to stay sated. He'd said it with such a poker face, as if he hadn't devoured two bodies in the woods today.

She was safe.

She was safe, and these stupid tears wouldn't stop coming.

Made no sense. She was glad Derek was gone. He would never hunt her again thanks to Gunner, and the Warlanders, and Damon Daye.

But she couldn't shake the feeling that something was wrong.

She took a sip of her wine, set the glass back down, and rested her cheek on her hand.

Corey pulled up and came to a stop. She got out and stared at her. "Was it you?"

"Was what me?" she asked innocently.

"The news footage. The fires. The dragon?"

"I don't even know the dragon," she said. Lucia had told her to keep quiet, so she would.

Corey came and sat beside her, looked at her face, and then reached across and cupped her cheek. "That black eye is going to be rough in the morning."

She huffed a breath, wiped her eyes with the sleeve of her hoodie again, and looked away. "I'm free."

Corey was quiet for a while. She leaned her shoulder against Hallie's and rested her head against her neck, stared at the woods with her. "I don't want to know, and I don't care. I'm glad you're free. You deserve to be happy, Hallie. None of that should've ever happened to you."

Her cousin kissed the side of her head and then stood, went inside, and left Hallie out here waiting for Gunner to show up.

He didn't.

After another hour, she picked her phone back up and texted him again. *Where are you?* Send.

****

Where are you?

Gunner saw the notification on his phone from the mount on his motorcycle. He read it three times before he slowed and turned his phone off. He coasted for a couple of minutes, lost in his own head.

He'd never been able to leave the territory until now, and he couldn't look back.

Hallie was safe from Derek, but he couldn't go falling for a woman who had been in it for a bite.

He couldn't do it again. He'd barely survived the first time.

Gunner hit the throttle on a straightaway, and his speedometer climbed.

100

125

152

168

192

Around 200 his mind went quiet, and there was the secret. If he went fast enough, if he got close enough to not existing anymore, nothing hurt anymore.

Stupid bear, getting hooked again so fast. All he knew how to do was destroy, and bond to the wrong women. He was best at falling for women who were just looking for a way out.

That's all he was—a way out.

Not anymore.

He never wanted to come back to Damon's Mountains again. Like Hallie, he was going to start over and find somewhere new. Maybe make some new friends. Find a new place to work. Find a house somewhere, and try his damndest to never look back.

FIFTEEN

Six days.

Almost one week.

Gunner opened the fridge in his apartment and pulled out a bottled water, sank onto the couch, and took a long drink of it. This was the hardest part of the day, where he thought about shouldering the satchel of clothes he kept packed, getting on his motorcycle, and driving back to the place that was calling to every part of him.

He'd always dreamed of leaving Damon's Mountains, but it wasn't like he'd imagined.

His phone sat face-down on the coffee table, plugged into a cord, charging.

Maybe today would be the day the text messages

waned.

He flipped over the phone, and the first text message that came through said, *You're an asshole.* It was from Lucia. She sent him the same text every day at the same time, as if she had an alarm set to remind her to ruin his day.

He huffed a laugh and shook his head. She would give up on him eventually.

He scrolled through the others. Mom and Dad, of course, even though he talked to them every night now. Damon had asked where he'd gone. Lucas had sent him a selfie of him and Kru and Landon shooting him the middle finger.

The last one had the smile fading from his face though.

Bash had texted, *Something is happening*, with a link just like he'd done a week ago, the night Hallie had disappeared.

With a frown, Gunner sat up, set the water bottle on the table, and clicked the link.

It led him to Hallie's social media page. Stupid Bash. Gunner already checked this every night. Secretly.

Hallie hadn't posted since her messages for

Derek.

Only when he opened up her page this time, there were new posts. She must've done these today while he was on job interviews.

After her posts to Derek a week ago, she'd put up a picture of her and Lucia and Cadence and Jenna, laughing together in a corner booth at some bar.

What the fuck? She was hanging with the Warlander girls?

He scrolled through those pictures, and it was Hallie with the happiest smile. His heart hammered against his chest.

She was out there. She was making friends and making memories.

Attagirl.

The next post was of her in the bleachers of some dirt-track car race, holding a tumbler that read *C-Team*. Blurred in the background were familiar faces from Damon's Mountains, and her cousin, Corey, cheering on the cars with her.

The caption read, *I've been livin' lately. About damn time.*

Gunner ran his hand down his jaw and scrolled up to the next post. She was standing next to the for-sale sign on 1010 Winding Creek Way. She was rolling her eyes heavenward, with this pretty smile painting her lips. There was mostly-healed, green bruising under one of her eyes. Derek must've smacked her during that abduction. Gunner clenched his fist and closed his eyes to control the rage that roared through his head. He wanted to kill that motherfucker all over again. Three steadying breaths, and he forced his eyes open to study the picture again. Her hair had blonde highlights in it now, and she had it curled in loose waves down her shoulders. She looked so good. Happy, even. The caption read, *I went to make an offer on this place so I could finally put down some roots and be neighbors with my cousin, but someone beat me to it.*

Holy shit. It was him. He'd made the offer on it before he left.

His entire body was rigid as he scrolled to the next post. It was a black-and-white video in slow motion of them on his bike, zooming away. It was edited to look like one of those old, grainy movies. The caption read, *Dear GW, my cousin told me something last night. She said she mentioned a bite to you. SHE mentioned it, not me. That was never my plan. That's not what you are to me. To me, you are just freedom, and I'll never feel differently. I just want another ride with you.*

His heart hammered against his chest.

Fuck.

Gunner set the phone down fast and linked his hands behind his head, stared out the window of the tiny, weekly-lease hotel room he was trying to force himself to love. GW was him. Gunner Walker. She was talking to him.

She didn't want the bite?

Why had Corey told him that then?

Had he been wrong?

Stupid hope flooded his middle, shredding his resolve to stay away from her.

A text came through from Bash. *Go outside.*

Gunner stood slowly, eyes trained on that text. He read it a few times just to be sure. Hope, hope, endless hope was all he could feel right now.

Gunner yanked open the front door and bolted down the hallway to the elevator. He hit the button over and over, but it was taking too long. He ran to the stairwell and sprinted down the three flights, then straight out the front lobby door. He didn't need to scan the parking lot. He knew she would be by his motorcycle.

Hallie wore a tight black T-shirt and ripped-up black jeans over some heeled leather boots. Her hair was tied back, and her eyes were rimmed with tears. She didn't smile. She looked uncertain, and he knew he'd done that to her.

Chest heaving with his breath, he strode toward her.

"Stop," she whispered, holding her hand out. "I want to say a few things."

"Hallie—"

"Please," she whispered thickly.

Gunner nodded, heart aching that he'd made her cry.

"Bash gave me your location. I'm not a stalker. I just wanted to have a conversation with you before you throw me away, so you can know exactly where I stand, and I can figure out exactly where I stand with you."

"Okay," he rumbled. The bear was already in his voice.

"It was messed up that you left like that," she said. "If you choose to be my friend after this, that's not how we are going to handle things. We aren't going to run. I do understand. You think I don't want to run? You're terrifying, Gunner."

"I don't mean to scare you."

"Not your bear, Gunner. I love your bear. I love what he did for me. I love what he is capable of. I love that he set me free." Her voice faltered on the last word, and she took a few seconds before she continued. "You feel very important, and to me, love is giving someone the chance to hold your heart, and to destroy you. Love was manipulation, and pain, and pretty apologies for things that would never change. And then you came along and in such a short amount of time, you taught me something different. And then you ran."

Fuck, he couldn't feel any lower. He hated that he'd hurt her.

"I was angry," she whispered. "And hurt, and there was this voice in my head saying this is just how it was. That's what men do." She lifted her chin higher into the air. "That's not what you're going to do. Not to me, and I won't do it to you."

He nodded.

"One last thing. The bite? Corey brought that up

to me one night. I didn't join in or agree or even say that was a good idea. I argued it. I don't want to be anyone other than myself now. Human, fragile, damaged. But I'm also hopeful, and healing, and growing, and getting to watch my old self come back little by little, and that's because of you. I'm not here for any reason other than I feel like my best self around you." The tears that had been building fell to her cheeks. "I like you, and I like myself with you, and I've changed my mind, Gunner. I think that's how love is supposed to be."

Gunner swallowed hard and asked, "Can I hug you now?"

"Really?" she asked, her dark eyebrows lifting high.

He laughed and rushed her, picked her up and crushed her to him, walked her backward slowly as she wrapped her arms tightly around his shoulders and buried her face against his neck.

"I'm sorry," he said.

"I know why you did it. I know, Gunner."

She was so small in his arms. He rubbed his cheek against her head and gripped her hair gently, swaying them slowly. He let off a long breath and closed his eyes, just existed here with her.

She'd said love. It wasn't just him in this. He wasn't alone in this bond. It wasn't like the first time. She wasn't using him, she wasn't just trying to get over someone.

He wasn't collateral damage.

She truly cared about him.

"I bought 1010 Winding Creek," he said gruffly.

"I know," she said thickly, clutching his shirt in her fists. "I was so happy."

"Yeah?" he asked, setting her back on her feet so he could look in her eyes.

"Lucia and the girls told me all about how important that number is, and that you would've seen it as a sign." She slid her hands up his chest and rested them there. "Lucia saw you there months ago."

Gunner's mind shorted out. "What?"

The smile that stretched across Hallie's face was the prettiest thing he'd ever witnessed. "She told me to tell you something."

"What's that?"

Hallie's eyes went soft. "You're getting warmer."

Chills lifted the fine hairs on his arms. "You want to go on a ride with me?"

"Depends. Where to?"

"Home."

Hallie's face crumpled, and she dropped her gaze. Two tears made little stains on the concrete near her feet. She nodded, and he hooked a finger under her chin and lifted that pretty gaze back to his.

"No more hiding. I won't let anyone hurt you. You can be the exact woman you want to be. No more running for either of us."

She slid her arms around his middle and rested her cheek against him, hugged him up tight.

"No more running."

SIXTEEN

"Watch out!" Gunner called.

Hallie ducked out of the way of a falling wall. As the dust settled around her, she dragged her gaze up to Gunner.

"I swear to everything, I'm going to get one of the girls to Turn you."

She giggled and brushed debris off her legs. "Lucia and Cadence already offered. Do you want me to be a tiger, or a bear?"

"Wait, what?" Gunner asked from where he was scooping the remnants of the dilapidated old cabin into the bucket of the tractor.

"What would you prefer?" she teased.

He cut the engine of the tractor. "That's not

funny."

"I'm pretty sure Lucia and Cadence were not joking. Remember that day I accidentally cut myself at work, and it was still bleeding when we met up with the Warlanders? They went all protective on me in the bathroom and told me to choose."

"Oh my God, we aren't talking about this right now. I need you to step away from the cabin, you are stressing me out. But also, smile. You look fuckin' cute and I'm going to take a picture."

She laughed and adjusted her hard hat, pulled her thick gloves farther up her forearms, and struck a pose as Gunner held his phone up and took a photo of her.

"Where did you get the tractor from?" she asked as she approached it.

"Kong."

Well, that shocked her. "Kong, your ex-boss?"

Gunner was wearing a white T-shirt smudged with dirt, jeans, and work boots. He looked so handsome leaning toward her in the seat of that tractor. "Maybe now he's my current boss."

"Stop," she said, stunned. "You're joking."

"I found out this morning."

"Gunner!" She whooped, climbing up into the seat with him. She threw her arms around him and couldn't stop the happy laughter that bubbled up out of her chest. "You got your job back."

"I got a different jobsite. New crew, new mountain, new machinery. He said I have one chance to prove myself as foreman again."

She pursed her lips against an emotional smile. "When do you start?"

"Monday. I wanted to surprise you over dinner tonight, after we were done demoing the cabin. I'm apparently terrible at surprises. Well…" He lifted his chin and said mysteriously, "Some surprises."

Hallie frowned. "I don't know how anything could get better than the news you just told me. I'm so freaking proud of you."

"It's going to be a long journey gaining back Kong's trust in me."

"You're going to do it. I know you will. And I'm going to be your biggest cheerleader."

Gunner pulled her closer and nipped at her neck. "Bear."

"Bear what?"

"I choose a bear if you're Turning, but you aren't

getting Lucia's crazy bear."

"I'll get your crazy bear instead?"

He chuckled and said, "Maybe. Someday." And then he twitched his head toward the one-lane dirt road that led up to this clearing. "If you were a shifter you could've heard them coming."

"Who?"

He grinned and helped her off the tractor, then pulled her by the hand to face the road, where a truck crawled up the hill to the clearing. It was Kru's truck.

With a baffled feeling fluttering in her chest, she waved to Kru and Cadence in the front seat, and when Lucia, Jenna, and Landon climbed out of the bed of the truck, she laughed and waved bigger.

The Warlanders were here, other than Lucas.

"What are you doing here?" she said through pleased laughter as she ran to greet them.

"We brought food," Jenna said. "Figured we should make memories for the first night you two stay up here."

"Oh, we aren't staying up here. We're just demolishing the cabin. We don't even have a tent or anything. Just starting work on this place."

The girls exchanged glances she didn't

understand. "What?"

From the back of the truck, Landon tossed a beer to Gunner, and then to Kru.

"Where's Lucas?" Hallie asked. He was always with them when they all hung out.

"He doesn't want to be in Gunner's territory. They still hate each other," Lucia said. And then she cracked a smile. "If you were a shifter, you would hear the lie in that."

A low rumble sounded through the trees, and Hallie froze, listening.

"What is that?" she asked as a flock of birds took flight from the trees in their woods.

"Lucia told your secret," Gunner said from behind her.

With a frown, Hallie turned. He was standing between Kru and Landon, his head cocked, his bi-colored eyes soft on her.

"What secret?"

"Once upon a time," Lucia said. "You spent the night with us because you were so sad that Gunner had left. You were lonely and you wanted to be around his people, and you drank one too many fruity beers, and you said that your dream was to live in a place like ten-ten someday. With Gunner."

Hallie jerked her attention back to Gunner, then to the opening of the road, where a semitruck appeared.

Her mouth fell open as she saw what it was dragging.

"No," she said softly, denying what she was seeing.

Lucas was driving the semi that was hauling the 1010 replica from Smashland Mobile Park to the clearing and the land she and Gunner were building a life on.

"Gunner wanted to buy it for you," Jenna said softly.

Hallie squatted down, overwhelmed as she watched Lucas pull the cream-colored single-wide with the green shutters to the space Gunner had been leveling all morning. Now that part made sense. Cadence squatted down next to her and put her hand on her shoulder. "Once upon a time, I wrecked a man. I didn't mean to, but I did it, and then you came along and put him back together. You deserve all the good things, Hallie."

Jenna was squatted beside her, eyes rimmed with

tears. "I thought we were going to be the ones to save him, but it was you."

Hallie wiped her eyes and turned to Gunner. Lucia stood near him, smiling at her. "Do you want the list now, or later?" she asked Gunner.

"What list?" Gunner asked.

Lucia pulled a folded piece of paper out of her back pocket and offered it to Gunner. "The list of people who have applied to be in your new Crew."

Gunner looked baffled, and shook his head slightly. "My new Crew?"

"Damon is expanding his mountains. You weren't meant to be under Lucas and the Warlanders, and for a reason. You're an Alpha, Gunner. I saw it months ago, and it was so hard not to tell you. You had to make the right combination of decisions to make it here, to this moment." Lucia gestured to the replica of 1010 as Lucas eased it into place. "You're supposed to make your own story."

"Who all knows?" Gunner whispered, his eyes full.

"Damon. Kong. Bash…everyone," Lucia said with a thick laugh.

"What if I mess it up?"

"You will," Lucia assured him. She smiled and

tipped her head toward Hallie. "And then you two will fix it."

Gunner dragged his stunned attention to Hallie. There were a thousand uncertain thoughts in that handsome gaze, but when he parted his lips and uttered the words he wanted to, Hallie already knew what he would say.

"Stay one more day."

She blew out a trembling breath and tried to control her emotions. "And then what?"

He nodded, and she knew they were in this.

They were all the way in.

Whatever happened from this moment on, they were in it together.

Damon Daye was growing his territory, and this was the beginning of the new Crew.

"And then we'll see."

More Books with These Characters

Warlanders

Warlander Silverback
(Warlanders, Book 1)

Warlander Beast Cat
(Warlanders, Book 2)

Warlander Grizzly
(Warlanders, Book 3)

Up Next:

Fastlander Fallen
(Fastlanders, Book 2)

About the Author

T.S. Joyce is devoted to bringing hot shifter romances to readers. Hungry alpha males are her calling card, and the wilder the men, the more she'll make them pour their hearts out. She lives in the PNW with a giant, tattooed hunkyhubby, a make-shift family, a herd of awesome kiddos, plenty of farm animals, and devotes her life to writing big stories. Foodie, bear whisperer, chicken-momma, thief of tiny bottles of awesome smelling hotel shampoo, nap connoisseur, romantic comedy fanatic, and bite-sized cattle rancher.

Bear Shifters? She's got 'em.

Smoldering Alpha Hotness? Yup yup!

Sexy Scenes? Fasten up your girdles, ladies and gents, it's gonna to be a wild ride.

For more information on T. S. Joyce's work,
visit her website at
www.tsjoyce.com

Printed in Great Britain
by Amazon